Blood Royal

Ian Robert Bell

Published by New Generation Publishing in 2023

Copyright © IAN ROBERT BELL 2023

All characters and events in this story are the product of the author's imagination and have no connection with actual persons living or dead.

The author asserts the moral right under the Copyright, Designs and Patents Act 1988 to be identified as the author of this work.

All Rights reserved. No part of this publication may be reproduced, stored in a retrieval system or transmitted, in any form or by any means without the prior consent of the author, nor be otherwise circulated in any form of binding or cover other than that which it is published and without a similar condition being imposed on the subsequent purchaser.

All characters and events in this story are the product of the author's imagination and have no connection with actual persons living or dead.

ISBN: 978-1-83563-051-8

www.newgeneration-publishing.com

New Generation Publishing

Acknowledgements

The author wishes to thank Deepa Shetty and David Doncaster for all their help and support over the years and for being good neighbours.

PROLOGUE

London Daily News
Billionaire's Daughter goes Missing
By Charles Cooper
London Daily News
Tamara Sheridan, nineteen-year-old daughter of American property tycoon, Randolph G. Sheridan, has been reported missing while attending university in London, England. A spokesperson for the Metropolitan Police stated that there was as yet no news concerning her whereabouts and the likelihood of her having been kidnapped for ransom has not been ruled out. Miss Sheridan was last seen on Wednesday evening, enjoying a night out in London's Soho district with some friends from her college. The weather was foggy, and Tamara seems to have become momentarily separated from the group of friends she was with. A close friend who was with her at the time said: 'It was really weird. One moment she was there and the next minute she was gone. We heard the sound of a car driving off down the road, but there was no sign of Tamara anywhere. It was just as if she'd vanished from the face of the earth.' A representative from London University revealed that Miss Sheridan was studying for a BA degree in Theology and Religious Studies, and had

just begun her second year at college. The university authorities are growing increasingly concerned for her safety, given the current level of knife crime and gang-related violence in the capital, and the ever present threat of terrorism on the streets of Britain's cities.

1

Flight: AA 6135 — New York/London Heathrow
Tuesday 9 October 2018

Simon Barrett gazed wearily out of the passenger window of his aircraft as it came in to land at Heathrow airport, lending its sleek black shadow to the earth below. Checking his wristwatch, he adjusted the dial to British time and sat back in his seat. 'Thank Christ for that,' he muttered under his breath; only another twenty minutes to go and then he could check in at customs and take a cab to his hotel.

In all his thirty-seven years, Simon had never been much of a flyer, preferring instead to drive, or take a Greyhound bus interstate whenever his work as a private detective required it. The passenger seats had been comfortable enough in business class, but after having been in the air for well over five hours, he was beginning to wish he'd taken on an easier job than the one he'd been offered and which had occasioned this particular visit to London.

It seemed over half a lifetime ago since he'd boarded his flight in New York and even longer since his meeting with Randolph G. Sheridan at the tycoon's luxurious penthouse apartment in Central Park. Simon recalled the meeting vividly. It wasn't often he went to a prospective client's home on business. Usually, his client came to his bland little office on the fourth floor of the Telford building where his secretary,

Marlene, would prepare them both some coffee and then exit the room discreetly while discussions commenced. But the meeting with Randolph G. Sheridan had been different. For the first time in his professional life, Simon had felt that he wasn't the person calling all the shots.

Mr Sheridan was a man in turmoil. Barely six days ago, his only daughter, Tamara had been reported missing while attending university in England and he had yet to receive a ransom note or any news of her whereabouts.

Randolph G. Sheridan — or 'George' as he preferred to be called — was no newcomer to acts of kidnap and extortion having once been kidnapped himself while attending summer camp as a child near the exclusive Rocky Mountain resort of Aspen, Colorado. That time, his own particular rescue had warranted the full attention of the FBI and Pinkerton's Detective Agency, and it hadn't been long before the kidnap gang had been bluffed and busted into submission, allowing the young Randolph to return to the bosom of his loving and ever-so-wealthy family in Vermont.

However, this time things were different. This time, it was his only daughter who had gone missing, and she had gone missing in a foreign country far away across the sea. As he had explained to Simon during their meeting that day in New York, the FBI hadn't been able to get anything out of the British authorities concerning his daughter's disappearance and were reluctant to extend their investigations any further inside the UK on account of some previous misdemeanour by a US marshall on British soil which had resulted in the deportation of two of their best operatives from England and a rather sniffy letter being dispatched to Washington from the Home Office.

Realising he wasn't going to get anywhere with the

British government using orthodox means, Randolph had decided to hire the services of a certain private detective he'd once used to spy on his estranged wife, Laura Anne in order to avoid paying the extortionate alimony payments he knew she'd screw him for in the divorce courts. Indeed, Simon Barrett had done such a good job of stitching up the former Mrs Sheridan, that Randolph had even kept Simon on a small retainer, lucrative enough to secure his services whenever he might need them. And now he needed Simon's help desperately.

'What do you know about the British, Mr Barrett?' was all Randolph Sheridan had asked of Simon as the two men gazed out across Central Park that afternoon, admiring the view from the rooftop garden of the Sheridan penthouse.

'They drink tea, play cricket and worship the National Health Service,' Simon replied trying hard not to sound too sarcastic.

Hearing this remark, Randolph made a sound in his throat that resembled something between the yelp of a hyena and suppressed human laughter before continuing: 'As you know, Mr Barrett, my daughter Tamara went missing in London last Wednesday evening and I'm prepared to pay quite handsomely for news of her whereabouts and safe return.'

'Then, why not use the British authorities, Mr Sheridan? Surely they know the score in their own country far better than we do.'

'Because for some reason, Simon, the *British authorities* aren't being very helpful. I don't know why exactly, but I've been in business long enough to smell a cover-up and I don't like it.'

'Didn't your daughter have a minder while she was in the

UK?'

'I offered to provide her with one but she wouldn't have it. Too young and headstrong, I suppose.'

'So, when did you last hear from her?'

'She phoned me the day before she disappeared. She sounded a bit confused and distracted, but didn't give me any indication that she was in any kind of trouble. In fact, she was in quite an upbeat mood, telling me she'd recently joined some religious organisation or other.'

'What kind of *religious organisation*?'

'Oh, just some Christian evangelical thing. She was studying theology at college, so I guess that's where she must have heard about it.'

'I see. And what was the name of this organisation?'

'She didn't say. Leastways, I can't remember. There's so many of them around these days.'

'Hmm. Pity. It would have been helpful if I had a name. I'm assuming you are not in any way a religious man, Mr Sheridan?'

'Hell no, I'm a fucking Democrat for God's sake! Can't be doing with that sort of thing. Mark my words Simon, those damn Jesus freaks will be running this country next if we don't watch out.'

'And your daughter — she was a practising Christian?'

'Yes. She developed a religious streak in her mid-teens and it never went away.'

'Better than drugs and Heavy Metal…'

'Uh…? Oh, yeah, I suppose so, but I'm worried about her all the same. She sounded very strange in that last phone call of hers. She was on medication you see and kept complaining of these visions she was having.'

'Visions...? What sort of visions?'

'Hallucinations I guess. Her doctor said it might be schizophrenia and that her meds would take care of it, but they didn't.'

'What happened?'

'The visions became steadily worse and more frightening in their intensity. She claimed she was being followed by demons and all sorts of crazy stuff like that, but she wouldn't elaborate on it. It's all a load of bullshit I know, but I'm concerned she may have had something on her mind and didn't want to tell me about it. Either that or she didn't want me to get involved — well, you know what young people are like. Anyway, whatever the case, I'll give you every assistance you require in order to find her.'

'Well, it might help matters if you could provide me with a brief description of Tamara. I recall that when we last did business, Mr Sheridan, your daughter was attending a private school in Switzerland, so I never actually got a chance to meet her. A photograph would come in useful if you have one to hand.'

'Yeah, yeah; sure,' replied Randolph, removing a small picture from his wallet. 'This is her. It was taken while on vacation in Florida a couple of years ago before she went to England — long oval face with shoulder-length ginger hair. A redhead, just like her mother.'

'Oh, right... good,' said Simon examining the photograph. 'You don't happen to have any other pictures of your daughter, do you? The more images I have of her, the easier it will be to make a positive ID.'

'I've got a few press cuttings. One of them is quite recent. Just last month in fact.'

'That's great. Can I see it?'

'Well yes, but... oh, never mind. It's in my study with the rest of the Sheridan archives. Why don't you make yourself comfortable in the living room while I go and fetch it?'

The Sheridan living room was very large, very classical and had a high ceiling which gave the place an atmosphere of airy grandeur and restrained elegance. Although a millionaire many times over, Randolph G. Sheridan was not the sort of man who flaunted his wealth. True, there was the almost obligatory collection of Mondrian and Picasso paintings which so infest the apartments of the super-rich the world over, and even a Roman portrait bust or two, but other than that, the room was practically devoid of ornament, unless of course you included the dazzling sunburst display of Wild West handguns which hung on the wall above the fireplace. Presently, Randolph returned clutching a leather-bound file full of press cuttings open near the middle of the binder:

'It's not very flattering, but it's the most recent image I have of Tamara. It's from the British press and dated two weeks before she went missing. Here, see for yourself.'

Shock wasn't an adequate enough expression for what Simon experienced the moment he clapped eyes on the newspaper cutting. Where, only a few minutes before, he had seen the fresh-faced image of Tamara Sheridan smiling out at him from the Florida photograph, he now saw the thin, pinched features of a brain-fucked crack addict emerging from the doorway of a London nightclub giving a two-fingered salute to the world.

'Is that...?'

'I'm afraid so, Simon. It's one of the reasons why I called you in on the case. I know you've had some experience with this sort of thing before,' replied Randolph, his voice trailing off into a sibilant whisper, 'only it looks like she's gone and gotten herself involved with the wrong sort of crowd. Either that, or she's gone anorexic on me, which personally I doubt.'

'Where was this picture taken?'

'It's a place called Fotheringay's — a nightclub in the Soho district of London. An old friend of mine was over in the UK on business and spotted it in the morning papers. It's some sort of alternative venue frequented by a wide cross-section of society and celebrity types. It's also where the London Punks and Goths tend to hang out. I gave her a right old tongue lashing about it over the phone but she just hung up on me and didn't get in touch again until her very last call on Tuesday. I haven't heard from her since.'

'Who are the other people in the photograph, Mr Sheridan?'

'Dunno — brat pack, I guess. Tamara never mentioned any names to me. You know what young people are like… Oh, hang on — yes, now I come to think of it, there were a couple of people… both women. One was called Rebecca Hamilton and the other went by the name of Abigail Pearson. Probably some student friends of hers.'

'Anyone else?'

Randolph creased his brow in recollection. 'Mmm, well now you come to mention it, there was someone else.'

'Who?'

'She didn't say, but one thing she did mention was the fact that she believed she was being stalked by someone.'

'Why didn't you tell me this before, Mr Sheridan?'

'Because Tamara was ill, Simon! She wasn't right in the head. She was coming out with that sort of shit all the time.'

'And what happened then — after she told you about the stalker, I mean?'

'She put the phone down on me and hung up abruptly as if she was being followed or something. I think she was calling from a phone box.'

'Didn't she have a mobile?'

'Yes, of course she did. Probably couldn't get a signal out or her battery needed recharging or something.'

'... Or she didn't want the call tracked. It's a trick some criminals use if they've got any sense.'

'Are you suggesting that my daughter may have been involved in some sort of illegal activity, Simon?'

'No, Mr Sheridan. Just an observation that's all. It's more than likely there's a simple explanation why she used a payphone. Either that or she was suffering from one of those paranoid delusions you mentioned. Anyway, at least I've got some names to be going on with when I begin my enquiries in London. What may be of more significance, however, is the fact that the British press seem to be extremely interested in your daughter for some reason. I know the Sheridans are a high-profile family and all, but you're not that well known outside the United States. Why the media focus on Tamara all of a sudden?'

'Ah, I was coming to that point, Mr Barrett. It would appear that Tamara had recently developed certain contacts among the upper reaches of the British establishment.'

'Such as?'

'Here, take a look at this other newspaper cutting,' replied Randolph, turning the pages of the binder over a couple of times. 'This photo was taken at a polo match in Windsor Park only this summer. It's from a British tabloid dated August 10.

Recognise the guy on the right, standing next to my daughter and the other two girls, Rebecca and Abigail?'

Simon stared at the second press cutting for a few moments and shook his head. 'Can't say that I do, Mr Sheridan. Who is it?'

'His name is Clive Meredith. He's an Anglo-American entrepreneur and philanthropist. Made all his money in the UK property boom selling prime real estate to foreign investors. You know the sort of thing I mean, Russian bigshots seeking to launder their capital into British landbanks. Shit like that.'

'You mean, Tamara was…'

'A high-altitude networker, Simon. This guy, Clive, is also into religion in a big way, which probably explains how he met my daughter. Apparently, he bankrolls some evangelical organisation in the UK, or so I've been led to believe.'

'So, what was Tamara doing slumming it up at a dive like Fotheringay's nightclub if you don't mind me asking?'

'Ah, but that's the mystery of it, Mr Barrett. That's what I want you to find out. And then I want you to find my daughter.'

2

'I want to go home,' said the girl with the ginger hair and American accent. She was sitting on a sofa in the corner of the room glaring defiantly at the man who had just offered her a cigarette. There were two men in the room. The one with the cigarette packet, and the other, the smaller of the pair who just kept glancing nervously out of the window through a gap in the curtains to the street below.

'I want to go home,' the girl repeated, taking the cigarette as the man clicked his lighter and lit it for her.

'Sorry, but we've got our orders, kid. It's nothing personal you understand. Just business.'

The man by the window withered him with a look. 'The boss said no talking.'

'She's nervous.'

'Not our problem. Tell her to smoke her cigarette and shut up or I'll put the gag back on. Our contact should be here with the money soon and we can hand her over.'

'You wait till my father hears of this,' the girl exclaimed. 'He doesn't mess around. He'll send someone to find me… and it won't be the cops.'

The man by the window smiled and looked at his watch. 'It won't be long now,' he said dropping the curtain closed. 'The boss is in a hurry with this one.'

'What's he want her for?' enquired the other man curiously.

'How should I know. Linda didn't say…'

His words were interrupted by the sound of a motorcycle engine throbbing in the street outside. Then the sound ceased abruptly as if the engine had been switched off.

'That must be them, Derek,' said the man with the cigarettes.

'No it's not. Linda said they would use a van, not a bike. In any case, who would use a motorcycle for a collection? Fancy a coffee?'

'Don't mind if I do. What about the girlie… What's your name again?'

'It's Tamara… Tamara Sheridan; and no, I don't want a coffee, thank you.'

'Suit yourself. It's instant anyway. Probably not in your league.'

A couple of minutes went by before Derek returned with two steaming mugs of coffee, handing one of them to his companion. Then the two men sat back and relaxed in the armchairs beside the sofa. The girl's feet were tied. She wasn't going anywhere.

'October already,' remarked the taller man to his friend. 'What are you getting your boy for Christmas, Derek?'

'Dunno, Lenny. He says he wants an Xbox, so this little job should see to it. How about you?'

'Sharon wants an air rifle. You know what girls are like these days.'

'Yeah, you fucking bet!' put in Tamara. 'If this was America you'd both be fucking dead by now!'

'Put a sock in it, kid,' said Lenny, tilting his head lazily in Tamara's direction. Evidently, he was in some sort of cannabis trance and his movements were becoming slow and languid.

'Give me back my mobile or I'll scream.'

'Now, why would you want to do that? No one can hear you anyway. This whole apartment block is unoccupied. It's scheduled for redevelopment soon. The boss is just using this flat as a safe house until he can sell the place.'

'Give me my mobile!' the young woman demanded, narrowing her gaze.

'No can do,' said the man called Derek, placing her phone face up on the coffee table in front of him. Reaching inside his jacket pocket, he produced an elderly automatic pistol. The girl flinched. She'd never seen such an antiquated weapon in actual use before and wondered what make it was. Then she remembered that guns weren't that easy to come by in England and reckoned it must have been one passed around the underworld for a fee. How old it was could have been anyone's guess. Privately, she hoped it would blow his hand off if he ever had to fire it.

SMACK!

The man brought the butt of his gun down on Tamara's phone, smashing the screen instantly.

'You… you'll pay for that!'

'Sorry luv. Mobiles can be traced. I should have thought of that earlier. Glad you reminded me.'

Tamara slumped back into the sofa. She would have to think of something else.

'Look,' she said, sitting forward again. 'You guys both want money, right?'

'Yeah,' replied the taller man who called himself Lenny. 'What's your point?'

'Okay, so here's the deal, Lenny. You let me go and I'll see to it that my dad pays you both a big reward. That way, we all get out of this mess in one piece. I get to go free and you don't do serious time. Why do this for some bigshot hustler when you can have all the money for yourself?'

Lenny looked at Derek and then back at the girl: 'Because if we did that, lady, our lives wouldn't be worth jack shit. The people we work for don't mess around. You got the picture?'

Tamara had to admit that she hadn't quite got the picture and thought of the nearest thing that made any sense. 'You mean like the Mob over in the States?'

'Something like that, kid, only our lot are a bit more hardwired into the system than yours and they've been around for a whole lot longer.'

'So, who's your boss then? The guy who owns this building?'

'He's nothing. Just the middle man.'

'Then who's in charge.'

'We don't get to know and Linda won't tell us.'

'Who is Linda...?'

Lenny glanced at his accomplice only to be met with a slow and deliberate shake of the head. Evidently, the matter was not one for discussion. Just then, there came the sound of heavy footsteps ascending the stairwell outside the apartment.

'That must be our contact now,' exclaimed Lenny, getting out of his chair. 'I'll let them in.'

'No you don't,' said Derek concealing his weapon in the side pocket of his jacket. 'Ask them for the password first.'

Lenny nodded and walked over to the door. 'Who's that?' he enquired, listening for an answer. There wasn't one.

'What's the password?' he continued nervously.

Still no answer.

Derek tensed and rose up out of his seat, one hand resting

on his gun. The silence was heavy with imminence. Something was wrong.

'What's the password?' repeated Lenny, a little louder this time so whoever it was on the other side of the door would hear. For a moment there was a pause when nothing happened. Then—

Tamara heard the sound of splintering wood. Saw the shattered door suddenly fly open with Lenny staggering backwards clutching his face as an eerie, lean shadow entered the chamber silhouetted against the amber glow of the hallway light beyond.

'Oh, Jesus,' she whispered under her breath as Derek drew his gun. 'Oh, Jesus…'

At the sight of Derek's gun, the eerie lean shadow halted momentarily and stood with legs apart on the carpet as if waiting for his next move. Now it was possible for Tamara to glimpse a bit more of the mysterious intruder and what she saw chilled her to the bone.

It seemed to be a young white woman, that much she could tell, but there wasn't much in it as the person she was now seeing more resembled a tall, skinny youth than anything remotely feminine. With greasy black hair tied in a ponytail and wearing nothing but a faded T-shirt, leather motorcycle jacket, blue jeans and biker boots, she stood motionless on the rug with one hand hovering just above her waist like an old-fashioned gunfighter. Not a *modern girl* at all.

Tamara had never seen such hard features on a woman before. Beneath the long, broken nose, her lips were set into a thin, cruel line that looked as if they had never raised a smile in decades. She couldn't see the woman's eyes. They were concealed by a pair of mirrored sunglasses that reflected what little light there was back into the room. *Beguiling* was the word that came into Tamara's mind as she regarded the mysterious stranger standing there in the doorway. But even as Tamara thought these things of the enigmatic woman in the motorcycle jacket, she somehow knew that she was in the presence of a hardened killer and that someone was going to die.

'You've got something I want,' said the woman in the black leather jacket. Her voice was dark and husky as if she'd smoked one too many joints and drank more whisky than was good for her. Instinctively, Derek backed off, levelling his pistol at her torso. The woman obliged him by raising both her hands in surrender, but Tamara could tell it was only a trick.

'She's broken my nose,' groaned Lenny still clutching his face.

'Shut up,' snapped Derek, not taking his eyes off the woman for a second. From the tone of familiarity in his voice, Tamara could sense that he knew who this woman was and didn't want to take any chances.

'Back off,' he said, gesturing at her with his gun.

'Anything you say, sonny,' replied the woman shifting her position only slightly. There was a scar on her left cheek but it was neat and clean-looking as if it had healed a long time ago.

'What are *you* doing here?' Derek asked, his voice now wavering on the verge of panic. Lenny wasn't too happy either, and Tamara could see him making his way softly towards the door in the vain hope that he wouldn't be noticed.

'I've come for the girl,' was all the woman said in reply, tilting her head to one side with a lazy, confident swagger. Tamara bit her lower lip and drew her knees up to her chest in a defensive posture. She knew this wasn't going to end well.

'Who told you we were here?' continued Derek, gripping

the handle of his pistol as if it were the last thing on earth.

'That's my business,' answered the woman running her tongue along the edge of her lip, 'but do you mind not shooting me in the stomach? It's by no means certain that you would kill me and I've got a terrible ache in my guts from a curry I had earlier on. If I were you I'd go for a head shot. It's the only way of killing a thing like me.'

'Shut up you animal,' said Derek raising his gun and levelling it at the woman's head.

Oh my God, he's losing it, thought Tamara clutching her knees closer to her chest and staring wide-eyed at the scene developing in front of her. Lenny was closer to the door by now and more determined than ever to make his escape from the room. Evidently, the concept of honour among thieves was not one that was closest to his heart right now.

It happened fast when it came.

The woman threw herself hard at Derek's waist, and Tamara saw the flash of a 9mm bullet as it ripped through the air and embedded itself in the wall behind her. The woman's velocity carried both combatants across the room where they crashed into a tall, freestanding bookcase and continued grappling for control of the weapon. She was strong, thought Tamara, but the man was putting up some stiff resistance, more out of fear and blind panic than anything else. Of young Lenny there was no sign. He'd made his exit from the room almost as soon as the fight had started and was probably legging it off down the road by now just as fast as his feet could carry him.

Tamara watched as the woman took hold of Derek's wrist, but then she saw him twist the gun towards his opponent in an attempt to gut-shoot her. 'Shit, that does it!' said the woman, pushing the gun back towards him and pressing the barrel against his chest. There was a muffled report as the gun went off drenching the woman in blood-splatter.

She held his limp body for a few seconds before lowering it to the floor and letting it roll away from her. Then she wiped the blood from her face, licked her fingers clean and turned her attention to the captive girl seated in the corner of the room.

Tamara squirmed uneasily on the sofa as the woman approached. Now that she was able to get a close look at her rescuer, a cold chill ran up her spine. There wasn't a single trace of humanity about this woman, whoever she was. Her skin was as pale as death, parchment white beneath her jet-black hair. Then the woman produced an ebony-handled switchblade and Tamara yelped with fear, prompting the woman with the knife to raise a finger to her lips for silence. Reaching down, she cut the rope securing Tamara's feet and pressed the blade back into its clasp.

'Who are you?' whimpered Tamara, terrified out of her wits. 'What's your name?'

'My name? If you knew that you'd be as damned as I am,' replied the woman as she removed what remained of the rope from around Tamara's ankles.

'Are you from the British security services?' continued Tamara, still curious to know who the woman might be and who she worked for.

'No; no I'm not.'

'Who sent you then? Was it my father?'

The woman stood up and looked at Tamara. 'Let's just say that I was sent by *higher powers* and leave it at that, shall we?'

'Oh, I see… It's classified is it? So, what happens next?'

'Next? Well, I don't know about you, but I'm going home to take a shower, put my feet up and make myself a nice hot cup of tea. I reckon I've done enough damage here for one evening, don't you?'

3

Simon Barrett had been filled with a sense of foreboding ever since his plane had touched down at Heathrow. Exactly why he was feeling so apprehensive upon setting foot in England he couldn't say, but the sense of apprehension had not lifted throughout the entire time his taxi had taken to drive him to his hotel and showed no sign of diminishing even though it was now getting on for nine o'clock in the evening, and he'd been in the country for the better part of a whole day.

He was also without his gun. In the States, he was registered to carry a firearm and quite often did, depending on the circumstances of the case in hand. Sure, the Feds had pulled him over on a number of occasions, but the phrase: *"It's okay officer. I'm a private detective,"* was usually enough to get him off the hook with nothing more serious than a strong verbal warning and a covetous glance at his shiny, nickel-plated .38 Magnum. The gun had cost him the better part of $1,600 dollars and packed considerable intimidatory value out on the mean streets of his native America. Over here in the UK, however, it would only land him with a night in jail and immediate deportation back to his country of origin; a thing that had to be avoided at all costs. If he needed some artillery later on, he could always secure himself a handgun and some ammo from the London lowlife of the area should the need arise. From what he'd heard, crime was pretty rife on the streets of the capital, and getting his hands on a basic shoot'n' chuck shouldn't prove too much of a problem. Indeed, as his client, Randolph G. Sheridan had said to him just before he boarded his flight to England: *"Seek all the information you need from among the ranks of the London underworld, Mr Barrett. On no account must you contact the British authorities on anything other than the most casual of terms."* When Simon had asked why precisely he shouldn't begin his enquiries regarding the disappearance of Tamara Sheridan with the police at Scotland Yard, Randolph had replied somewhat cryptically: *"Just be careful, Simon, that's all I'm saying. You can get in touch with me by phone at my ranch out in Montana where I'll be staying for the next few weeks. And use a payphone — I don't want any of the calls to be traced."*

He'd made the wrong decision in taking on the case, hadn't he? All the signs were there right in front of his eyes but he'd been too blind and too stupid to see them — a strange foreign country on the brink of anarchy; the sinister shadow of organised crime; a missing millionaire's daughter and a dodgy New York tycoon who didn't want to get the local police involved. Christ, but the whole thing stank like a fresh dog turd on a wet road and he'd just gone and stepped right in it. This, plus the fact that his landing at Heathrow airport had been delayed for over ten minutes owing to a terrorist alert should have warned him from the very outset that he'd got himself unwittingly involved in something way too far above his head.

Still, at least his hotel was comfortable enough, thought Simon as he cast a glance around his room. Randolph G. Sheridan had been as good as his word and booked him into one of London's top hotels. *"You'll be staying at the Noyland,"* he remembered him saying; *"It's better than most places and a lot less elitist than Claridge's."*

Well, he was right. The room Simon had been allocated was a small suite on the second floor. It had its own reception lounge, complete with two armchairs, a sofa and the biggest plasma screen television he had ever seen. There was a smaller one in the bedroom, opposite the bed on which he was now reclining, idly flicking channels with the TV remote. There wasn't much too see apart from a few old films and a documentary about the Second World War. Unable to concentrate on the latter programme, his thoughts soon returned to matters of more immediate concern.

He was out of his depth and he knew it. This sort of case was one best left to Scotland Yard or the FBI. He simply didn't have the resources or the experience to handle it. Sure, spying on a cheating partner was one thing, but jumping on a plane at a moment's notice to go looking for a missing little rich girl was quite another. Heaving a sigh, he raised himself from the bed and wandered over to the minibar to fix himself a drink.

Pouring out a miniature bottle of Jack Daniel's, he downed it in one gulp. The calming effect of the alcohol was immediate as it swirled around his mouth and disappeared down his throat, prompting him to pour out another and take it over to the bed where the TV was still on, blasting out the final death throes of the Third Reich as if it had happened only yesterday. Muttering an oath, Simon picked up the remote and pressed one of the channel buttons at random. There was a moment's pause while the screen went blank. Then:

The scene opened out onto a vast auditorium, its interior packed with row upon row of seated figures, all with their eyes fixed on the stage in front of them. Behind the stage was a huge concert hall screen showing the familiar image of a smiling, bearded Christ underscored with the phrase, Eternal Life

Ministries in big, bold electric graphics that rippled hypnotically in front of the huge capacity crowd. Simon had seen this sort of thing before in his native America. It was a religious broadcast aimed at spreading the word of God to the masses. Religion was big in the States, and judging by the size of the audience assembled in the concert hall, it was beginning to take off in England too. Taking a sip of whisky from the perspex tumbler beside his bed, Simon looked on as the lights went down and a spotlight hit the stage. Presently, a figure walked out from the wings accepting rapturous applause from the crowd. It was a handsome, middle-aged man dressed in a pale blue suit, his auburn hair neatly parted to one side. The applause grew in intensity until shouts of 'Hallelujah!' and 'Praise the Lord' echoed around the walls.

The man is Clive Meredith, charismatic leader of the Church of Eternal Life. It is he they have come to see.

Simon didn't recognise him at first. From a distance, the man looked like any other evangelical preacher he'd seen on prime time TV back home. The airwaves were full of the shit and he was just about to reach for the off-button when something caught his attention. He'd seen this guy somewhere before.

Clive Meredith raised his hands and the crowd became silent, hanging on his every word. Pausing for effect, he beamed a warm benevolent smile at the multitude before beginning his sermon. Well, it wasn't so much a sermon as more of a ten-minute psychobabble aimed at pummelling the crowd into submission before the real work of emptying their wallets began.

There's one born every minute, thought Simon, taking another sip of Jack Daniel's from his rapidly emptying glass.

Then he noticed something else. The smiling image of Jesus on the screen began to fade, only to be replaced by the face of the man on stage. His nose was straight and long, the cheekbones well defined, but his wide cosmetic grin did not extend to the pair of predatory eyes that nestled beneath his expertly threaded eyebrows.

But that wasn't all.

Beneath the computer-generated image was displayed the man's name — Clive Meredith, patron of the Church of Eternal Life in England. Simon recalled where he'd first heard that name. It was the same person in the press cutting that Randolph Sheridan had showed him in his apartment in New York. The photograph taken in Windsor Park earlier in the year along with Tamara and a couple of other girls in the frame who Simon also recognised from another photograph Randolph had shown him depicting Abigail Pearson and Rebecca Hamilton, two of Tamara's student friends. Now, they might be worth talking to, thought Simon, making a mental note to contact Tamara's college first thing in the morning before he picked up the remote and flicked channels for the evening news.

The news was about a shooting in an apartment block in the London district of Croydon. The victim was male and he'd been shot in the chest at point-blank range. There was some talk of a contract killing and possible gangland involvement before the next item of news came on and Simon decided to call it a day. Turning off the TV, he rolled off the bed and ventured into the bathroom to clean his teeth. He'd get a good night's sleep and see how he felt in the morning. One thing was certain. The case he was working on wasn't going to yield up its secrets that easily without an awful lot of footslogging on his part. Maybe a chat with Tamara's two university friends might reveal something. Well anything was worth a try.

***

'Good to see you're hard at it,' commented DI Keith Reynolds as he walked into the CID room at West End Central police station. 'Where's everyone else?'

'We're a bit pulled out at the moment, sir,' replied DC Brady glancing up from the screen. 'It's the cuts. Not enough manpower to go round.'

It was true. Only two of the desks in the room were actually occupied by real flesh and blood detectives, while what remained of the team were either out patrolling the streets, languishing on sick leave or just not there any more.

'Same old story, Susan. Got anything on that Croydon shooting yet?'

'Not a dickey bird, chief. One of the locals reckons he heard a motorcycle in the street around the time of the incident, but that's all. Whoever did it must have been a professional. Either that or a chancer who just got lucky.'

'What about the type of weapon used?'

'The medical examiner hasn't had time to extract the bullet yet and there's no trace of the weapon in the immediate vicinity. Can we talk about something else instead?'

'Like what?'

'The Tamara Sheridan case for starters. Anything happened with that?'

'No, and it's not likely to either. The man assigned to the job has been moved to another investigation.'

'Such as…?'

'The Vinny Jackson case.'

'What — that little twat who was caught chucking the acid?'

'Yes. It's all over the news. There's been quite a spate of it recently and the politicians are demanding something done about it. He was only fifteen apparently.'

'Christ, fifteen and a pimp already?'

'Well, they start younger these days, Susan.'

'Who was telling you?'

'Inspector Lefarge.'

'Oh, that old dinosaur. I thought he was putting in for retirement.'

'He was, but he changed his mind at the last moment. Sense of duty I suppose.'

'Sense of duty, my arse. He's old school. Probably earning too much money taking bribes from the poker dens.'

'I dare say, but his knowledge of all the old manors goes back a long way. Maybe he's just trying to tie up a few loose ends before he goes.'

'Hmm, maybe. Talking of loose ends, there was one development concerning the Croydon shooting that I forgot to mention.'

'Really? Tell me.'

'Well, it might be nothing, but apparently a guy called Lenny Mitchell walked into Vine Street nick a couple of hours ago spilling his guts about the fact he knows who did it.'

'Who?'

'He wouldn't say. He was in a highly agitated state, demanding full anonymity and round the clock protection before he bubbled.'

'What happened?'

'They had to let him go. He wasn't making much sense.

Just kept rambling on about vampires, people in high places and the fact he needed to get out of the country if the matter ever reached the tabloids and his name was mentioned.'

'Sounds like a nutter to me, Susan. We get them all the time.'

'Yes, but he's a nutter with plenty of form. DC Davidson was checking him out on the police computer earlier on. Apparently, Lenny has a bit of previous for running extortion rackets on the Euston Road.'

'Your point?'

'He seems to have had some association with Linda Bailey and her crew…'

At the mention of the name, DI Reynolds furrowed his brow, regarding his colleague with a look of concern.

'Bring him in, Susan — and make it fast!'

4

Tamara had never ridden on the back of a motorcycle before and certainly never one this big. She could feel the breeze in her hair as the huge, low-rider muscle bike crossed Tower Bridge, its driver heading south at a steady cruising speed before turning off into a series of narrow side streets that were typical for that area of London.

My, but she was skinny, thought Tamara, her hands clasped tightly around the woman's torso. Even though the driver was wearing a black leather jacket, Tamara could feel the woman's bony ribs as she moved in the saddle every time the bike took a bend in the road. She was cold too. Icy cold, just like the night breeze that was blowing off the River Thames to their left. It wasn't long before the bike came to a halt outside a large roller-shutter door that formed the entrance to a tall, old-fashioned warehouse building which towered above the street to a height of about five storeys.

'We're here,' exclaimed the woman, bringing her motorcycle to a halt and kicking the footstand of the bike down hard with the heel of her boot. Dismounting from the bike, she walked over to the shutter door and produced a set of keys from her jacket pocket. Inserting one of the keys into an electronic lock, she pushed a large red button with the palm of her hand. There was a short pause before the metal shutters began to rise, revealing the interior of a derelict loading bay inside. Glancing briefly up and down the road, the woman returned to her motorcycle, revved the throttle and drove inside with Tamara still perched astride the pillion seat of the bike.

'We go up here,' said the woman, turning off the engine and pointing to a flight of concrete stairs.

Obediently, Tamara followed her mysterious rescuer up the stairs as if it were the most natural thing in the world. The thought that the woman had only recently killed a man hardly entered her mind as they both ascended the staircase, eventually coming to a stop outside a sturdy reinforced door which the woman proceeded to unlock with a security key.

'This is my place,' said her rescuer pushing open the door and flicking on a light switch. 'You should be safe enough here for the time being. Take a seat and make yourself at home. We might be here for quite a while.'

'How long is a while?' enquired Tamara curiously.

'For as long as I deem it necessary,' snapped the woman. 'If you want a drink and something to eat, the kitchen is over there. Don't think of trying to escape. The door locks automatically and it's a long way down to the street. Now, if it's okay with you, I'm going to take a shower and wash some of this blood off me. Bye for now.'

Tamara watched as the woman left the room. Then she looked around. It wasn't what she expected of a warehouse. The place was furnished with a collection of quality antique furniture of the kind only people as wealthy as her father could afford. A large, ornate chandelier hanging from the ceiling by a length of chain provided the only source of illumination in the room. Other than that, the vast cavernous interior of the chamber was cloaked in shadow and covered in dust. Evidently the place hadn't been cleaned in decades.

For some reason, Tamara's eyes were drawn to a window high up in the wall at the far end of the room. Instinctively, she walked over and pulled up a chair. Standing on the chair, she was able to look out through the window down into the street below. It was too far to jump and in any case, the window was secured by four vertical bars set into the wall with huge iron bolts. No chance of opening that, she thought, climbing down from the chair and continuing with her investigation of the room. It wasn't long before her gaze fell upon a long sofa. The sofa was partially covered with a scattering of books, newspapers and magazines, some of which had cascaded down onto the beautifully patterned Afghan carpet that covered the floor. A low table in front of the sofa was similarly festooned with magazines and newspaper cuttings which shared a similar attraction to the floor as their cousins on the sofa. Picking up one of the magazines, Tamara noticed that it had a picture of Jimmy Carter, a former president of the United States on the front cover and that the pages of the magazine were yellow with age. The date on the cover was December 1979, well over thirty-eight years ago, but that wasn't all. There were even earlier newspapers and glossies from the 1970s scattered about, including one showing the face of a young woman staring out from the second page. The woman had ginger hair just like Tamara's, only it was styled differently in the fashion of a mid-1970s teenager. She bore a strong resemblance to the woman with the motorcycle, except that that woman's hair was black and fairly long and she wore sunglasses. Someone had drawn a solid black line around the newspaper article with a marker pen. Clearly, the girl in the picture held some significance for whoever had drawn the line.

'She was called Julie Kent,' came a voice out of nowhere.

Tamara put down the newspaper and turned to see her rescuer standing in the doorway. She was dressed in a grey silk kimono embroidered with swirling Chinese dragons the colour of smoke. Her hair was hidden by a white towel piled on top of her head turban-style. She was still wearing her mirrored sunglasses.

'Who was Julie?' was all Tamara said in reply. For some reason, her legs had become weak at the knees, forcing her to sit down on the sofa.

'She was me,' said the woman with a mischievous grin. 'Julie Kent was me.'

Tamara looked back at the photograph then turned to the woman once again with a puzzled expression.

'But this newspaper is dated 1977...'

'Well spotted, Tamara,' continued the woman, leaning against the doorframe. 'That's the year I went missing... just like you.'

Tamara regarded the photograph once more and began reading the article below:

"... 'Julie Kent,'" echoed the woman who was by now standing behind Tamara looking over her shoulder as she read, '"went missing in July 1977 while visiting the Roxy nightclub in London with some friends." It was the height of the Punk era and I was nineteen.'

'Impossible. That would make you almost sixty by now and you don't look a day over twenty. How come?'

The woman moved round and sat on an armchair facing Tamara.

'Well, you've seen all the movies, haven't you?'

'What do you mean?'

'Oh, you know the sort of thing — *Dracula; Night of the*

Living Dead, all that sort of shit.'

'I don't follow.'

'The undead, Tamara. I'm one of the undead, and you nearly became one as well if I hadn't kicked the door in back there and settled that fucker's hash with his own gun. You really should be more careful you know.'

Tamara looked at the newspaper photograph once more. It was true; the girl in the picture did indeed bear a strong resemblance to her rescuer. The jawline was the same and she could have dyed her hair black, but the eyes would surely clinch the deal. She couldn't see the woman's eyes because of the sunglasses she was wearing.

'Take your sunglasses off,' she demanded firmly rising to her feet.

The woman shook her head slowly and also stood up. 'You really don't want me to do that, Tamara. You really don't.'

'Take them off!' yelled the young American reaching across to yank the shades off the woman's face. A sharp smack sent her rocking backwards on her heels and back down onto the sofa with a thump. For some reason she found herself sucking her thumb. It was something she hadn't done since she was three.

'Why have you brought me here?' she grizzled, forcing back her tears.

'It's for your own good, Tamara. If I hadn't rescued you from those two men, you'd be halfway to hell by now.'

'But I'm a practising Christian. I can't go to hell.'

'That's what they all say,' replied the woman in a sing-song voice, her face lighting up with a smile as she snorted a huge line of cocaine straight off the coffee table as if it were the most natural thing in the world. 'Want some?' she exclaimed, offering Tamara the bag.

Tamara shook her head. 'I don't take drugs.' She was lying of course but the woman just ignored it.

'Very sensible. Nasty habit.'

By now, Tamara had stopped sucking her thumb and was sitting forward on the sofa with both her elbows propped on her knees and her chin cupped in her hands.

'Why won't you show me your eyes?' she said inquisitively.

'Because the last person to look into them went stark raving mad,' the woman replied firmly. 'I trust that answers your question.'

Undeterred, Tamara continued with her interrogation, confident that her family connections were the sole reason for her kidnapping and that the woman — whoever she was — just wasn't giving her the full story.

'Who were the two men?' she exclaimed. 'The ones holding me prisoner in the apartment. Who were they? And don't say they were vampires. I'm not buying it.'

'They weren't. They were mortals just like yourself, but they were working for one. A senior vampire called Sir James Silver to be exact.'

'*Sir* James! Has everybody in this country got a bloody title including the undead?'

The woman laughed, showing way too many teeth. Then she removed the towel from her head and shook out her hair which cascaded over her shoulders as black as midnight.

'All senior vampires usually bear a title. Some vampires are centuries old and it reminds them of the world they used to inhabit when they were young. In actual fact, Sir James' street name is Jimmy Silver. He used to have knighthood back in the eighteenth century but it lapsed with his mortal death in the 1780s.'

Tamara frowned. She didn't believe a word of what the woman was saying but went along with it anyway just to see if she could find out anything more about her current predicament.

'Who are you working for, *Julie?*'

'I told you before. My name isn't Julie Kent.'

'What is it then?'

'Sterling. My name is Sterling. I adopted the name when Julie... I mean, my former self died.'

'When was that?'

'In 1977. It was the year I went missing. Julie Kent's body was washed up on a beach on the south coast, but when she came to, she wasn't Julie any more. She was me.'

'And do you work for a senior vampire then, *Sterling?*'

'No... I have no master.'

She's holding something back, thought Tamara growing more confident in the presence of her terrifying jailer. *There's something she isn't telling me.*

'Someone is pulling your strings, Sterling. Who is it?'

The woman looked away. 'I can't tell you that. It's classified.'

'Oh, so you're working for the British Intelligence Services after all. Well, I'm certainly pleased to hear it. So, when do I get to go home then?'

'You mean, America?'

'No. I mean my student flat in Hampstead. I've got a cat to feed and I need my meds. If I don't take my medication, I have a tendency to go a bit loony.'

'Your meds? Edward didn't mention anything about any medication.'

'It's none of your business. I've got a few issues with my head that need sorting out, that's all. And who is this Edward guy anyway? Is he your boss?'

Again, the woman looked away, realising that she'd said too much.

'Who… is… Edward?' Tamara continued, putting out her words slowly and deliberately.

'Edward is a high-ranking member of the Roman Catholic Church — a cardinal to be precise.'

'A cardinal!?'

'Yes, they're about the only people in this world that I'm shit-scared of if you must know. He's the man who ordered me to keep an eye on you over the last couple of weeks.'

The realisation slowly dawned in Tamara's mind: 'You're the person who's been stalking me…'

'It was for your own good.'

'How do you mean?'

The woman lit a cigarette and offered one to Tamara who accepted it without a word of thanks.

'There's no better way of saying this, Tamara. According to Edward, you have become a person of interest among our kind.'

'Your kind?'

'Yes, Tamara. It would appear that you have come to the attention of a senior vampire; one who will stop at nothing to accomplish whatever it is that he has in mind for you.'

'And what might that be precisely?'

'He wishes to breed with you.'

'Well he can fuck off.'

'It's not that simple, Tamara. Vampires have been hardwired into the power structure of this country for centuries. The aristocracy were always riddled with them, and in recent years they've spread out into the rest of society. The more influential among their number are capable of wielding a considerable amount of power and influence behind the scenes.'

'What are you trying to say?'

'What I'm trying to say, is that you've got to go to ground for a few days before we can figure a way of getting you out of the country and back to the States. There, I trust that answers your question.'

'No, it doesn't,' replied Tamara growing more pissed off by the second. 'I don't know what the hell is going on but I'm not buying any more of this crap. You're obviously working for my father. He never wanted me to come to London in the first place and he doesn't like me doing theology and religious studies at uni.'

'I don't think your father's got anything to do with it.'

'Shut up! You have to let me go. I've got an important meeting tomorrow with a man from the Church of Eternal Life. They want me to become one of their lay preachers. They say I've got potential.'

'I bet they do…'

'So, you let me go, okay?'

'If I released you now, Tamara, the only eternal life you'd be experiencing would be that of the undead, and personally I wouldn't recommend it.'

Seeing she was getting nowhere, Tamara changed the slant of her argument.

'You mentioned "we", Sterling. You said that I have to go

to ground for a few days before *"we"* can arrange to get me out of the country. Who are "we" exactly? Were you by any chance referring to the man you call Edward, or somebody else?'

'Yes, as a matter of fact I was. Tomorrow, I'm taking you to see a mate of mine in Islington. He's called, Jerry Skinner. We go back a long way.'

'Is he a Catholic priest as well?'

'No, he's a full-patch member of the Hell's Angels if you must know.'

'The Hell's Angels...' echoed Tamara to herself. 'Who are they?'

The vampire smiled and shook out her hair once more. She'd forgotten just how old she was.

'The Angels are a motorcycle gang, Tamara. They used to be big back in my time before they got busted by the feds.'

'Oh, yeah. I think my dad mentioned them once or twice. He's got a Harley Davidson you know.'

'I'm pleased to hear it, Tamara. Anyway, you're going up to Skinner's place to lie low for a few days. Skinner and his mates should be sufficient protection for you until we can work out a way of getting you clear of the UK without being detected.'

'But I've got a passport.'

'That's the problem. I don't know how far Jimmy Silver's influence extends these days. It's best not chancing it by using your own passport. You'll need another identity and that might take a bit of time.'

'What, you mean an ordinary citizen can compromise your passport control?'

'There's nothing ordinary about Jimmy Silver, Tamara,

and besides, England isn't like America. It's a one-party state run for the convenience of the British Establishment. If you're a member of the right club, you can more or less do what the fuck you like, and that includes getting the authorities to run a passport check on anyone of interest trying to leave the country — you savvy?'

Tamara gasped. She'd never expected such a state of affairs could possibly exist in "little old England" and was truly shocked. But then, she'd never anticipated finding herself kidnapped and then shut up in an old warehouse with a homicidal maniac called Sterling who claimed to be a vampire from the 1970s and who didn't look a day over twenty-one.

'I need my meds, Sterling,' was all she said. 'I need my meds.'

'Okay, I can get them from your flat up in Hampstead, but you'll have to give me your house keys. I don't fancy busting any more locks than I have to in one single day.'

'Here,' Tamara replied, reaching into her pocket. 'That's the front door key to the building and the smaller one is the key to my apartment. The landlord lives on the premises in a flat downstairs. He's a bit deaf. If he asks you who you are, just say you're a friend from uni who's come to check on the cat. He's called Roosevelt.'

'Who — the landlord?'

'No, the cat, stupid.'

'Oh… right. Sorry. Anyway, you'd best be getting some sleep, Tamara. I'm going out on the prowl if that's okay with you?'

'Where are you going, Sterling?'

'I have a bit of business to transact. When I return, I'll drive you over to Skinner's place and then I'll go and fetch your meds.'

'Don't forget, Roosevelt.'

'I won't.'

'Oh, and Sterling,' Tamara continued sarcastically, 'this bit of business of yours. It wouldn't have anything to do with turning into a bat and feasting on human blood by any chance, would it?'

'Of course not,' the vampire replied with a smile. 'I only ever drink black market hospital blood. Now, why don't you get some sleep while I'm out? You look like you need it.'

Tamara obeyed. Within a few minutes, she was curled up on the sofa fast asleep beneath a tartan fleece. She didn't hear the woman leave.

Sterling left the warehouse dressed in her faded blue jeans and black leather jacket. She did not take her motorcycle, preferring instead to strike out across London towards her destination on foot.

A fine mist had descended on the city by the time she reached the gentlemen's club in St James's which was where she wanted to be. Pressing the intercom button at the side of the door, she waited.

'Yes. Who is it?' came a voice from the intercom.

'My name is Sterling,' she answered, 'I have a meeting with Edward de Valois.'

The voice paused. 'Just a moment...'

There was a short interval of about fifteen seconds before she heard an electronic buzz followed by a click which told her the door was open.

'You may enter now,' came a different voice. 'Cardinal de Valois is upstairs in the library room. It's the third door along at the end of the corridor.'

She was not aware of the presence of many people in the building. It just wasn't that sort of a place. Climbing the stairs, she reached the first floor landing and turned left down a wide passageway that was flanked on either side with marble portrait busts of Roman emperors. Then she kept on walking, past the lounge bar and billiard room until she came to a set of double doors at the far end of the corridor. Here, the familiar scent of cigar smoke told her that someone was present in the library and that this someone was most likely the person she had come to see.

The rear of a wing-back leather armchair framed by an antique marble fireplace greeted Sterling as she entered the library. Seated in the chair was an elderly gentleman, cigar in hand, hunched over a large chessboard, totally absorbed in one of those complex endgames to which certain types of intellect can become easily addicted. It wasn't the Edward she knew for him to be seated like that with his back to the door of a public room — or any other room for that matter. All too easy for a potential assassin to slip a garrotte smoothly around his neck and then exit the building without so much as a whisper of suspicion. But she was wrong.

'You're late,' said de Valois turning round in his chair. 'Is there a reason for that?'

'I walked,' replied Sterling, regarding the man with a mixture of fear and respect.

'Sit yourself down,' said the elderly cleric pointing to a chair. 'I was just finishing off this interesting little endgame before you arrived. It's rather elegant, don't you think?'

'If you say so, Edward. I'm not much of a chess player myself.'

'But you used to be a fine musician,' continued the

cardinal placing a beleaguered black king firmly in check. 'Music is an activity which requires a high degree of intellectual stamina, does it not?'

'That was a long time ago… Before the change.'

'I know, I know — before you became one of the undead. It must be such a sad business to lose one's soul.'

'Are you joshing me, Edward?'

'Good heavens, no. Merely an observation, that's all. It's what people like me exist for Sterling — keeping you lot under control.'

'Since when have I ever been a threat to humanity, Cardinal?'

Edward reeled off a list of her victims then offered her a large brandy which she accepted coolly and without thanks.

'Okay, so I've topped a few mortals in my time. What vampire hasn't? But I was always sad about it.'

'Ha! That's what I've always liked about you, Sterling — your remorse. It shows you've still got a bit of humanity left in you. I can work with that.'

'Get to the point, de Valois. What's this meeting about?'

'The girl. How is she?'

'Tamara?'

'Yes. I trust she is well?'

'Of course she is. I've got her locked up in the warehouse until we can get her out of the country. I'll be moving her up to Skinner's place tomorrow.'

'Excellent. What about the kidnappers?'

'I was forced to kill one of them. The other got away.'

'Careless of you. Do you happen to know who it was?'

'A guy called, Lenny Mitchell. He works for Linda Bailey.'

'Thought as much. Linda is one of Jimmy Silver's main contacts in London.'

'Tell me something I don't know, Edward. The question remains, what does Jimmy Silver want with Tamara Sheridan?'

'It's like I told you, Sterling. He seeks to breed with her.'

'Why?'

'To create a vampire just as powerful as yourself. He is your vampiric grandfather after all.'

'So, why pick Tamara?'

'Because, she's a redhead just like you were when you were Julie Kent. According to folklore, redheads tend to make better hosts for vampires to use. It's got something to do with recessive genes, apparently.'

He'd never taken his eyes off the chessboard in all the time he'd been talking to her. It was just as if she wasn't there. She was about to say something when Edward looked up.

'Lenny will have to be terminated.'

Sterling nodded. 'How?'

'In the time-honoured way my little bloodsucker.' Reaching into his pocket he produced a small silver crucifix and handed it to her. 'Leave this with the body when you're finished. When Silver realises who it is that is on his tail, he'll most likely back off and leave Tamara alone.'

The vampire took the cross with a wince then regarded him strangely. 'Edward,' she said, 'it's been a long time. I need to feed.'

'Then you have my permission, my child. You may take what you require from Lenny but don't linger too long in the vicinity.'

'Why not?'

Edward glanced at the clock on the mantelpiece then looked at Sterling once again.

'There's no better way of saying this, my dear,' he said letting out a sigh.

'Saying what?'

'Owing to the increase in the number of vampires in Europe over the last thirty years or so, my political and religious masters have decided that it is high time your ranks were thinned out a little.'

'Meaning...?'

'Meaning, there's going to be a cull and it begins at midnight tonight.'

Sterling stiffened in her chair.

'Yes,' Edward went on, 'I thought that might alarm you. I'm sorry to be the bearer of bad tidings, but there you are. I tried to intervene with the Vatican on your behalf but I'm sorry to say that I was overruled. You'd better keep your head down and lie low for a few weeks. It's going to be a bloody business.'

Sterling swirled her brandy around in its glass then looked at Edward. 'You promised you would tell me the whereabouts of Jimmy Silver. I've still got a few scores to settle with him.'

'The last I heard of Jimmy was that he'd got wind of the cull and fled the country a couple of weeks ago.'

'Where did he go?'

'I don't rightly know. He's vanished off the radar, so to speak, but I know of somebody who might be able to help you find him.'

'Who?'

'Graveyard Mary.'

'Who's she?'

'Her real name is Marie Gibeau. She was a voodoo

priestess… and a damn fine poker player in her time.'

'Where can I find her?'

'Highgate Cemetery,' replied the cardinal, handing Sterling an old-fashioned iron key. 'She's been dead for well over a century and this is the key to her mausoleum. Oh, and you'll probably need this as well,' he added, fumbling around in his cassock until he withdrew a small leather-bound notebook. 'It's some instructions for the ritual you will have to perform once you enter the tomb.'

'A ritual… What for?'

'To wake the dead, of course. The dead know more than the living when it comes to secrets. Marie should be able to tell you where Silver is hiding, or at least how to go about finding him. Apart from that, I cannot help you.'

'Thanks a bunch!'

'Don't mention it, my dear,' replied Edward with a mischievous gleam in his eyes. 'Now, if you don't mind, I need to get a bit of sleep. There's none of us getting any younger and I've got a long day ahead of me tomorrow. Leave the book and the key with the porter when you've finished with them. We wouldn't want them to fall into the wrong hands now, would we?'

***

It was around midnight when a man with dark brown hair and wearing a navy blue fleece detached himself from the other pedestrians along Oxford Street and sauntered off down a short lane in the direction of Soho. He was carrying an overnight bag over his shoulder, but his plans for the evening were becoming more blurred with every minute that passed.

His face in the hard Soho light had gone quite pale and his eyes had taken on a worried, haunted look as he walked down the lane carefully dodging the discarded mixer bottles that littered his path. He knew *she* would come looking for him. Knew it with every fibre of his being. If only he could get out of town before dawn then everything would be all right. He could lie low for a while somewhere down on the south coast then make his way back to London in a few weeks' time. By then, the cull would most likely be over and she would be dead. *Yeah, good idea Lenny,* he thought to himself. *Get to the south coast, wait for a while and then come back. That's the best plan.*

Behind him he heard a slap and jerked his head round to see where the noise had come from. There, on the pavement, directly beneath a violently retching party-goer, a star-shaped pool of vomit was spreading itself slowly gutterwards. *Only that,* thought Lenny as he continued walking down the lane towards his destination. It was still a long way to the railway station and he'd have been better off taking a taxi, but for some reason he'd decided to walk.

Lenny was a creature of habit, and cocaine was one of them. He badly needed a fix, and if that meant missing the last train out of London then so be it. The Soho area was the best place to score a bag and that he firmly resolved to do before he did anything else.

At the end of the lane, Lenny turned left by Meard Street and quickened his pace. Then, about twenty metres up the road, he spotted what he took to be a woman wearing dark eyeshades and a black leather jacket walking towards him. To his immense relief, the woman brushed past him and continued on down the road, peering occasionally at the traffic as she went. Lenny stopped walking and stood still for a second or two, sucking in great gulps of air as his heart rabbited in his chest and his hands trembled. That was close, he thought. Too damned close!

He waited for a while until he saw the woman climb into a car and disappear from view. Then he walked on until he came to a flight of concrete steps which led down to the basement of a tall, red-brick Georgian house. In a matter of minutes the transaction was completed and Lenny re-emerged into the street clutching a small polythene bag full of white powder. Glancing round to make sure the coast was clear, he vanished up a nearby alleyway to sample the goods.

'Ah, that's better,' he exclaimed. 'Good stuff as well.'

He was about to take another line when something made him stop. He was being watched.

'It's been a long time, Lenny,' was all she said.

Slowly, Lenny turned his head and prepared to have his worst fears confirmed. No, it wasn't the prostitute. It was a sharp-faced white woman of about twenty-five years of age, though he knew she was a whole lot older than that. A cold drizzle had flattened her jet-black hair across her brow, partly obscuring her features, but the malevolent intensity of her gaze beneath those mirrored sunglasses of hers left Lenny under no illusions as to exactly who she was. For some reason he began laughing in a vain attempt to smooth the waters.

'Sterling — how are you me old mate? Long time no see!'

'Yes, it's me, Lenny,' she replied in a voice as hard as steel. 'I think we've got some talking to do.'

'Look, if it's about the girl…'

'What about her?'

'I had nothing to do with it. It was Linda who put me up

to it.'

'That's not important any more.'

Lenny looked about. There was no way out. Only a high brick wall at the end of the alleyway. He was trapped.

'Here, have some of this,' he said holding out his bag in the way of a peace offering. 'It's pure Columbian. The best...'

She was closer now, her arms extending towards him in the mock parody of a lover's embrace. He knew he was going to die almost as soon as her hands clamped around his throat. For a second, Lenny caught his reflection in her mirrored sunglasses then he went into a spasm and died. It was over.

Sterling smiled as she lowered his body to the ground and placed the small silver crucifix next to his head. Bending over the body, she extended her fangs and bit deeply into the side of his neck waiting for the flow. When it came, it was better than anything she'd tasted in a long while. Almost as good as A-class charlie, she thought as she crouched low on her haunches shadowing her kill like some giant bird of prey. She couldn't stay long in the vicinity. The cull would begin at midnight and then she would have to watch her back. If she managed to survive over the next few days it would be nothing short of a miracle. The Catholic Church was always scrupulous when it came to matters of genocide.

5

He'd drawn a complete blank.

It wasn't that the university authorities hadn't been helpful. They'd told him all they could about Tamara Sheridan but it wasn't enough. At least, nothing he could work with. All he knew so far was that Tamara had been an exemplary student who had handed all her course work in on time and never missed a lecture. Other than that, they couldn't say on account of Simon not being a real police officer but only a private detective from a foreign land. As her personal tutor, Doctor Murray had told him: "You could be anyone, Mr Barrett. We don't usually divulge any of our student's private details to strangers. It just wouldn't do…"

Wouldn't do…

That phrase. It was so very British, thought Simon as he walked out into the street from the university building, none the wiser for his efforts. That the college authorities hadn't been more forthcoming was understandable in the circumstances. All the same, there was something about Dr Murray he didn't like. It was the way the guy had avoided eye contact with him all throughout their conversation. In any other walk of life it could be interpreted as someone being deliberately evasive, but Simon couldn't be sure. Bernard Murray was an academic, and academics could be a bit like that, forever verging on the autistic end of the spectrum and with all the social skills of a housebrick. Maybe the old drone was just naturally shy; there was simply no way of telling and no way of penetrating the university system other than continuing to poke around on the campus until he got reported for stalking and escorted off the premises. What could he do?

Well, he could at least fix himself a coffee at one of the many sidewalk cafes that inhabited the area. There was one he'd enjoyed a bit of breakfast at earlier on in the day. 'It's just off Russell Square,' he murmured to himself checking his street map. 'Not far...'

It wasn't long before he found the place he was looking for. Going up to the counter, he ordered a medium Americano and a blueberry muffin then seated himself down at one of the small aluminium tables on the pavement outside.

So far, he had no leads as to the whereabouts of Randolph Sheridan's daughter and no clue as to what might have happened to her other than the fact that she had disappeared outside a joint called Fotheringay's nightclub while enjoying an evening out with some student friends — those same friends who were not available for interview, if what Dr Murray had said was anything to go by.

Then there was that religious organisation her father had mentioned — the one Tamara had recently joined. Now, that had to be the same one connected with Clive Meredith, the evangelical preacher he'd seen on the TV in his hotel bedroom the previous evening. What was it called again... the Church of Eternal Life or something like that? Yes, that was the name. He could certainly do with asking a few questions there, assuming he could locate the address in the UK where it operated from. Clive, however, might prove a bit more difficult to track down though. His sort usually were.

Taking time out from his problems, Simon bit into his

blueberry muffin and washed it down with a mouthful of coffee, savouring the flavour of the softened muffin as it vanished smoothly down his throat. He was just about to take another bite when his enjoyment was suddenly interrupted by a waspish feminine voice.

'Are you the bloke who's been asking after Tamara?'

'What?' spluttered Simon, turning to locate the owner of the voice; a thin, gaunt little woman bearing the image of a swallow in flight tattooed on the left side of her neck.

'Are you the geezer who's been asking after Tamara?' repeated the girl in a broad London accent. She couldn't have been much more than seventeen years of age, with light brown hair and wearing a hooded fleece with black leggings and boots to match.

'Yeah, I am,' replied Simon, taking a closer look at the girl. 'Who are you?'

'My name isn't important,' she answered, shifting nervously on her feet. 'I've been sent to warn you to get out of London. This town isn't safe for you.'

He hadn't expected this. At least, not so soon in the investigation and certainly not in a country like England. Instinctively, he reached for his gun then remembered he'd left it in America. 'Who sent you?' he asked, all his attention now focused on the girl.

'Nobody,' she replied. 'Just get out of London, that's all I'm saying.'

'Here, sit yourself down,' said Simon pulling up a chair. 'You want a drink?'

The girl shook her head and glanced around. Then she relented and sat herself down eyeing him warily.

'Coffee?' he asked raising his eyebrows.

The girl nodded.

'And would you like something to eat with it? A toasted sandwich perhaps?'

The girl nodded again, only more enthusiastically this time. It was clear she hadn't eaten in a long while. The needle marks in her forearm confirmed his suspicions. Someone was pulling her strings and using her drug habit to exert pressure on her. He would have to tread carefully.

'So, why do I have to leave town then? What's the problem?'

'You've been asking too many questions,' replied the waif between mouthfuls of toast.

'Questions? What sort of questions?'

'Questions about the American woman. The student who disappeared.'

'What about her? Do you know where she is?'

The girl was too quick for him. 'Just get the fuck out of England while you still can. There's stuff going on here like you wouldn't believe.'

'What kind of stuff?' continued Simon, truly astonished by the speed at which the girl had devoured her sandwich. Just then, a car drove by causing her to glance in its direction. Evidently, she was being watched.

'Look, I've got to go,' she said, depositing the crust of her sandwich back on its plate. 'I've done my job. You've been warned.'

Before he could catch her arm, the girl rose up from her seat and walked off quickly down the road. He tried to follow her but it was too late. Turning a corner, she gave him the slip, vanishing into the London crowds as if she'd never existed at all; nothing more than a figment of his own imagination and a salutary reminder that he was now involved in something way too big for an ordinary private detective like himself to deal with.

Peering into the distance, he tried to catch a final glimpse of the girl but she'd gone, leaving him with a hollow feeling in the pit of his stomach and the knowledge that he was now a marked man in a town he wasn't at all familiar with. It wasn't a pleasant thought.

***

The clatter of boots echoed along the walls of Stockwell underground station as a gang of fifteen or more teenagers and young adults swarmed up the station stairwell pushing aside startled commuters and barrier staff alike as they fanned out into the street, shouting and bawling expletives as they went. The commuters scarcely had time to recover their wits before an even larger crowd of young people — most of them male — clattered up the stairwell, following hard on the heels of the first group like a pack of wild dogs.

'It's the North London firms!' yelled a member of the first group to emerge from the station. 'Looks like it's on top for the lot of us!'

'We've been set up!' shouted another member of the group who went by the name of Jarvey. 'Wait till Sterling hears about this. She'll blow her fucking stack she will. This'll kick things off for sure with Tulloch's mob.'

'There's loads of them!' shrieked a young woman sporting a bleached blonde, Ska hairstyle cropped short on top with flowing sideburns.

Too late. The second group had just emerged in force from

beneath the station canopy and were already fanning out into the Clapham Road.

The girl with the spiky blonde hair heard someone grunt as they were hit with a pickaxe handle. Heard another of her associates split his brow against a brick wall. Saw the electric flash of blue denim as one of the stragglers from the first group hit the deck beneath a fusillade of kicks and blows, dark claret spilling from his scalp.

'We're fucking dead here, Debbie!' yelled Jarvey to the young woman with the spiky blonde hair. 'I reckon the coppers have got Tulloch in their pocket, getting his boys to sort out crime south of the river while giving him a free hand to tax the West End poker dens bone dry.'

'Bang go our profit margins then,' answered Debbie in reply.

'Fuck the profit margins! Get on your mobile and call for help. Things are starting to get hectic around here.'

'Okey dokey, shan't be a mo.'

Trembling fingers jabbed in the numbers and paused until a voice with a broad London accent came on the other end of the line.

'Hello. Who's that?'

'Orlando, it's me — Debbie!'

'Why didn't you use the code word?'

'Sorry, I forgot — "Blood Royal".'

'That's better. I almost hung up on you then. What's up, Debbie?'

'Orlando, we're fucked! There's loads of them. They came over on the Tube.'

'Who?'

'The North London mob! It's Tulloch's old firm and some

of the Stonebridge crew. We need help fast.'

'Where are you?'

'Stockwell underground station.'

'How the fuck did you get yourself caught up in a maul like that?'

'Well, me, Jarvey and some of the gang were out steaming the Tube. It was nothing much — just lifting a few wallets and stuff, when all of a sudden, we realise we're not exactly alone on the fucking train. About fifteen of Tulloch's boys had got on at the Oval and they swaggered into our carriage giving us the evil eye routine, so I whispers to Jarvey to spread the word that once the train pulls into Stockwell, we all make a run for it. And so we did, but there were more of them waiting for us on the platform, so then we—'

'I thought Sterling and Skinner told you never to go out steaming the Underground no more. The coppers have got things all tied down on that score.'

'We thought we'd give it one last try — well, you know what I'm like. In any case, it ain't the coppers we're dealing with down here.'

'Yeah, but it still won't go down well with her ladyship, will it?'

'I know, but what can I do? Jarvey thinks we've been set up by the police. He reckons they've got Tulloch to do their dirty work for them so they don't have to use the Special Patrol Units on account of the civil liberties brigade screaming blue murder about police brutality. That way, the feds can sort out crime this side of the river and the government gets to keep its nose clean. Personally, I think Lefarge is behind it all.'

'Who... Inspector Lefarge?'

'Yes, old George Lefarge. One of the sex workers from

Soho heard about it from Susan Brady — her what used to be in the Vice Squad. She's an old friend of Sterling's so I reckon it must be true.'

'What makes you so certain?'

'The tart in question was Stella Ferguson. Hers was the pimp who threw the acid at Jenny Hancock — right fucking mess she was in an' all. Anyway, according to Stella, Inspector Lefarge gets her pimp off doing time for it by smudging the interview and telling him all the right things to say in court so his case gets chucked. Sterling gets wind of what happened to Jenny and goes ballistic, grassing up Lefarge to his superiors at Scotland Yard. Then, old Lefarge pulls a few strings at his lodge and manages to worm his way out of it by a hair's breadth, but by now there's bad blood between Lefarge and Sterling, and all the gangs south of the river, including us lot in Southwark.'

'Ha, ha; bad blood, eh! That's a good description for the likes of Sterling.'

'Yes, Orlando — very funny, I'm sure. Unfortunately, it just so happens to have made us all flavour of the month with the Metropolitan Police. Lefarge is pulling in favours from Shaun Tulloch to even the score and make things look good for him in the eyes of Scotland Yard… Now what about giving us all a bit of back up down here why don't ya!!

6

The front door of the Hampstead flat was standing open when Sterling entered it and walked down the hallway towards the kitchen. Of Tamara's cat there was no sign. Only the half-eaten remains of a cat's dinner lying in a tray on the kitchen floor was all there was to suggest a feline presence in the room.

'Here, kitty kitty,' she murmured as she made her way softly through the flat. 'Here kitty kitty. Come to Auntie Sterling.' But it was no good. The cat just wasn't there at all, and it wasn't long before she found out why. There was a cat flap cut into the bottom of the kitchen door. Evidently, Roosevelt had made his exit through the cat flap and gone off on a jaunt of his own as some cats are prone to do. But why was the front door open and the lock broken?

Too bad, she thought. Tamara would just have to accept the fact that her cat had a mind of its own and leave it at that. The girl was lucky to be alive after all. If she had any sense, she'd forget all about her cat and concentrate on getting out of London as fast as possible before Silver's henchmen caught up with her. She'd be safe enough for the time being up in Skinner's place in Islington, but that could only be a temporary solution. If what Cardinal de Valois had said was true, then Silver would be pulling out all the stops to find her and drag her to his lair, wherever that happened to be.

Then there was the problem of the cull. According to de Valois, the cull had started at midnight, which was all of sixteen hours ago. By now, most of Europe would be crawling with legions of latter-day vampire hunters all intent on claiming the first kill. That meant she would have to watch her own back as well as Tamara's over the next few days, if she wanted to stay alive.

Alive... Sterling considered the irony of that word. She'd never been truly alive ever since that night back in 1977 when she'd become one of the undead. Of course, there were other vampires in the land considerably older than herself and a good deal more adept in the ways of her kind, but none were quite as cunning or as ruthless as she was. That was what Jimmy Silver feared the most about her. She was a threat to his power base that could never be ignored.

What the fuck!

She'd spotted him. The silhouette of a young man passing between two rooms across the hallway. There was someone else in the apartment.

Pressing herself against the wall, she became lost in shadow. Whoever the intruder was, he was quite expert in the way he just prowled around, scarcely making any sound as he passed from room to room. Evidently, he was a professional; but what kind of professional, she wondered — a burglar or a vampire slayer? It wasn't long before her questions were answered.

From her hiding place pressed up against the wall of the corridor, she could see a slender, masculine figure standing between the bathroom door and the entrance to the living room, its skin as pale as moonlight. The smell of old death hung in the air, telling her that whatever it was, it had been dead a long time. Silver had put another vampire on Tamara's trail and it had tracked her down to her apartment. Oddly enough, the thing standing there in the hallway was dressed in much the same vintage clothing as Sterling herself. Whoever the creature was when he had lived, he must have been a contemporary from Sterling's own generation. Curious, she moved from her place in the shadows, determined to get a better look at the stranger in the hallway. Sensing her presence, the thing jerked its head in her direction, baring its fangs with a hiss. Then it snarled and retreated down the hallway with Sterling in hot pursuit.

'Come here, dead boy!' she yelled, grabbing him by the shoulder. The creature growled, exposing its fangs once again as it turned on her, all the more desperate to escape than anything else. As she clamped her hand around its throat, Sterling got a better look at the face and was shocked to see how much it resembled a long-dead pop star from her youth. Then she drew out her silver switchblade and stabbed the thing repeatedly in the stomach until it let out a piercing shriek as the blade did its deadly work, sending the revenant into a spasm of shock that culminated in it falling to the floor and shaking violently like someone experiencing a *grand mal* seizure.

She always hated the next bit.

Apart from the occasional twitch, the body on the floor became still and motionless. Then, after a few seconds had elapsed, a series of thin, blue flames emerged from the corpse as it rapidly began to putrefy right there in front of her eyes. The stench was truly appalling.

Sterling turned away, shielding her gaze from the dreadful vision of mortality lying there in the hallway. It was every vampire's worst nightmare to die this way.

Of the body, nothing remained apart from a dark shape on

the carpet and a blackened layer of greasy soot on the ceiling and upper walls of the corridor. Walking into the bathroom, she looked around, checking to see if there were any cupboards. Seeing one with a mirrored door above the sink, she opened it and began rifling through its contents.

Bingo! She'd found what she was searching for. Tamara's medication. Three large blister packs of antipsychotic tablets. Quite high dosage too by the looks of them. Was Tamara really that close to the edge, she wondered? Oh well, it was none of her business. She'd completed her mission, found the medication, slain another of Silver's henchmen and failed to find the cat. Two out of three wasn't bad. Now it was time to bike it up to Islington and see how Skinner was getting on with Tamara. Boring her rigid with one of his ancient anecdotes more than likely. If he was, then the young lady would probably need her meds pretty damn quickly.

Pocketing the tablets, she made her way out of the bathroom towards the front door. It was a ground-floor flat with a small front garden. Walking briskly down the garden path, she turned into the road where her motorcycle was parked and almost bumped into a man coming the other way. The man made his apologies in an American accent and carried on walking towards the building she'd just come out of. Thinking nothing of it, Sterling straddled her bike and heeled the kickstart down, revving up the engine before driving off. If the man was another of Silver's goons come looking for Tamara, then he was in for a nasty surprise. The blackened shape on the floor would be ample reason for that.

The first thing Simon noticed when he entered the flat was the smell. His thoughts were that someone must be cooking sausages, so pungent was the scent of roast pork hanging in the air. Then he saw the shape on the floor. It was the shape of a man, down to the sprawled legs and single outstretched arm, outlined in grey crematorium ash as plain as day.

He could scarcely believe his eyes. Spontaneous human combustion! He'd first read about it when he was a kid in high school — folk who just burst into flames for no apparent reason, their bodies reduced to ashes in less time than it takes to boil an egg, and by a heat so intense that it could quite easily have consumed everything else in the room in a matter of minutes. And yet it hadn't.

True, there was some soot on the uppermost parts of the wall, but when he made to wipe it off with his fingers, he found no sign of burning underneath. The magnolia walls were as fresh as the day they'd been painted, and that wasn't too long ago, judging by the condition of the rest of the apartment. Who could have done this, he wondered? Or more to the point, *what* could have done it?

Then he had another thought. What if the shape on the floor had been Tamara? The very idea appalled him, especially when he considered that it would be he himself who would have to break the news to her father.

But there was something else. Why was there no police tape on the front door of the apartment and why had the front door been left standing open? Tamara had been reported as missing, and surely her flat would have been sealed off and carefully dusted down for evidence. Yet there was no sign of any police activity anywhere to be seen. At least not in the corridor anyway. Maybe a more thorough search of the flat would yield some clues?

Taking care not to step in the ash, Simon made his way down the hallway and began searching through the rooms.

They weren't what he'd expected of a student's residence, but then, Tamara hadn't exactly been your typical student. Light and spacious, the apartment had plenty of style and looked as though it had recently enjoyed the attentions of a cleaning lady. There wasn't a single speck of dust anywhere to be seen, unless of course you counted the abomination lying in the hallway, whoever that poor wretch might have been.

It's not Tamara. There would have been something in the press about it. Anyway, there's no such thing as spontaneous human combustion. It's a myth...

Going into the bathroom, he noticed the open door of the sink cupboard. Most of its contents had been decanted into the washbasin beneath.

This flat's been broken into. That would explain why the front door was ajar and why I didn't need a key from the landlord...

His thoughts were interrupted by the sound of a heavy motorcycle engine in the road outside. Thinking nothing of it, he continued his reconnaissance of the apartment, again stepping gingerly over the ash on the hallway carpet. He was about to go into the living room once more when he became aware that someone was watching him. Turning to face the open front door, he saw the silhouette of a figure outlined against the daylight. It was a woman.

'Yes, can I help you?' enquired Simon, sounding to all the world as if he had a perfect right to be there. The mysterious woman made no reply, but just kept on staring at him through her mirrored sunglasses, scarcely moving at all. It was then that he realised who this woman was. It was the same woman who had almost bumped into him in the street several minutes before. Why had she come back, he wondered?

'Can I help you?' Simon repeated, a small part of him hoping the woman was Tamara.

'Maybe you can,' replied the stranger in a voice loaded with menace. 'Who are you and what are you doing here?'

'I was about to ask you much the same thing,' replied Simon.

'Then why didn't you?'

'I... I don't know...'

His voice trailed off into a sibilant whisper. There was something about the woman in the ripped jeans, leather jacket and motorcycle boots that filled him with a sense of dread. Whoever she was, it was clear to Simon that she was no stranger to calculated acts of terminal violence. For some reason the word "carnage" popped into his mind, together with a series of mental images culled from several decades before; not a few of them clearly belonging to the mid-1970s where this woman must have had her origins. Strange though, how she didn't look very much older than a day over twenty.

'Who are you?' the woman demanded, her right hand hovering just above the pocket of her jeans. Evidently, she was packing a concealed weapon.

'My name is Simon Barrett and I'm a private detective.'

'American?'

'Yeah.'

The woman looked him up and down, checking him out.

'You've come looking for Tamara, haven't you?'

'Yes, yes I have,' Simon blurted out before immediately clamming shut again. He didn't know who this woman worked for. She might even be Tamara's killer for all he knew.

The woman glanced first at the ash on the carpet then looked back to Simon without giving any indication of surprise.

'Who was it?' he said, trying to keep his nerve.

'A vampire who should have known better,' the woman replied coldly and without a trace of emotion.

He knew she was telling the truth. There were no signs there to indicate anything to the contrary, but the implications tore at his guts. How could it possibly be true?

'It's not Tamara then,' he exclaimed half-jokingly.

'No, it is not, Mr Barrett.'

'Then who is it?'

'Like I said before. Someone who should have known better.'

'You…?'

The woman nodded. 'With this,' she replied pulling out her silver switchblade.

Simon gasped and took a step backwards, raising both his hands defensively. 'Look, I don't want any trouble. I'm just looking for Tamara like I said.'

'Who sent you?'

'Her father, Randolph G. Sheridan. He put me on her case because he wasn't getting anywhere with Scotland Yard.'

'That figures.'

'What do you mean?'

The woman smiled, revealing a row of sharp white teeth. 'The police won't be investigating the case, Mr Barrett.'

'Why ever not?'

'Because this is England, Simon and our police are servants of the Crown and not public servants as many would have you believe.'

'I don't follow you.'

The woman smiled again. It was a thin, cruel smile born

of bitter experience and long suffering. Privately, he wondered how old she really was.

'In England, the police obey their political masters. Am I making sense?'

'You mean they've been taken off the case?'

'Something like that.'

'But how? Tamara is a high-profile missing person. In America, the FBI would have been involved by now.'

'You're not in America, Mr Barrett. This is Britain... and we don't have an FBI. Come to think of it, we don't even have a written constitution, which basically means that any joker with a bit of influence can usually do exactly what they fucking well like and get away with it.'

'Like who?'

'Like the person who arranged to have Tamara kidnapped in the first place.'

'You know who it was?'

'Yes. His name is Jimmy Silver. He used to be called Sir James Blackthorne, but that was a long time ago.'

'When?'

'The latter part of the eighteenth century if you must know, Simon; and he really isn't someone you should be messing with.'

There it was. She'd told him the truth. Now she observed his reactions from behind her mirrored sunglasses. He didn't understand. Few mortals did the first time they were told. Quickly, she changed the subject:

'Can you ride a motorcycle, Mr Barrett?'

'What...? Er, no I don't think so. I've only ever driven a car.'

'Don't worry. You'll be a passenger. I'm doing the

driving.'

'Where are we going?'

'To meet Tamara of course. She is the person you've come to find, is she not?'

'You know where she is then?'

'Of course I do. I'm the person who rescued her from Silver's goons in the first place. Now come along Simon; we can't stick around here all day. Not with that thing lying there on the carpet.'

Simon followed her obediently out of the apartment. He didn't know why he trusted the woman or where they were going. She'd mentioned a place called Islington, but that might just have been a ruse on her part to gain his trust. He couldn't be sure.

'Who do you work for?' he said as they approached the large, low-rider motorbike that was parked outside in the street.

'Cardinal de Valois,' she replied, handing Simon a spare crash helmet before climbing onto the bike.

'You work for the Vatican?' he said incredulously.

'Cardinal de Valois is my friend. He just so happens to be a member of the Catholic Church, that's all.'

'But — *a cardinal?*'

'It's always a good idea for creatures like myself to know someone on the inside, Mr Barrett. You never know when it might come in useful.'

'I don't understand.'

'You don't have to. Here, climb on, Simon; and don't worry. I'm a good driver and this bike is one of the best. I borrowed it from a friend of mine.'

'Who — the cardinal?'

'No, stupid. A bloke called Jerry Skinner. He's the man we're going to see.'

'And what does he do?'

'He's a member of the Hell's Angels in case you were wondering. Got any more questions?'

'Yes, I have as a matter of fact. What's your name?'

'It's Sterling,' the woman replied turning round in the saddle before heeling down the kick-start of the bike and throttling the engine into life. As they roared off down the road, Simon's heart sank. He didn't know where he was going or what he would find when he got there. Everything was based on trust and the say-so of someone who was obviously a dangerous lunatic. Literally anything could happen.

7

'I left her with you, Jerry! Where the fuck is she?'

'I'm sorry, Sterling. It's like I said. We ran out of milk, so Tamara offered to go out and get some from the minimart down the road.'

'And you let her...?'

'I didn't think nothing of it, Sterl, honest I didn't. Islington ain't a bad sort of a place so I thought she'd be all right. Maybe she's met somebody she knows and they're having a coffee or something.'

'It's been over five hours, Jerry. She's gone.'

Simon looked on as Sterling paced the floor of the Islington apartment, glaring first at the man called Skinner and then at the young woman with the cropped, bleach-blonde hair sitting on the sofa. Her name was Debbie and she had a black eye.

'And what about this twat here,' said Sterling pointing at the girl with the black eye. 'Where'd you get that shiner from, eh, Debbs?'

'I walked into a door,' the girl replied without making eye contact.

'Oh, you walked into a door, did you?' echoed Sterling menacingly.

'No,' replied the girl... 'I didn't.'

'So, what happened?'

Debbie looked first at Skinner and then at Simon. 'Who's

that?' she said, changing the subject.

'His name is Simon Barrett. He's a detective from America,' Sterling replied curtly.

'A detective! What are you doing bringing him here for?'

'He's a private detective, Debbie. He was investigating the kidnapping of Tamara Sheridan, who I believe has just been kidnapped again thanks to Jerry here.'

'We don't know that, Sterl,' interrupted Skinner. 'She may just have met up with an old friend.'

'Thanks, Jerry. When I want your opinion I'll ask for it, okay? So how did you get that black eye, Debbie? You didn't say.'

Debbie looked at Skinner for reassurance. Skinner nodded, indicating it would be better to tell the truth than to try and bluff it out with Sterling. Reluctantly, Debbie began her tale of woe:

'Well, I was out lifting wallets from passengers on the Underground with Jarvey and some of the Southwark crew when we were attacked at Stockwell station by a gang of hards from North London. There was a fight and I got a black eye.'

'Great! So now you've gone and broken the truce it took me ages to set up with the North London firms.'

'I'm sorry, Sterling. Jarvey reckons the police had a hand in it.'

'That wouldn't surprise me, Debbie. Anyway, it isn't the only problem I've got at the moment.'

'Oh — what's up?'

Sterling knelt down and laid out two lines of coke on the coffee table before snorting them both up her nose with a rolled up banknote. Then she offered some to Simon, but he declined with a shake of his head, wondering what earth-shattering revelation she was about to reveal next. That the three people he was sharing the room with were all heavily into organised crime was more than apparent in the manner in which they spoke and the subject of their conversation, but what he couldn't work out was the connection with Tamara. It wasn't long before he found out.

'I've got to find her, Jerry. It's more than my life's worth.'

'What's happened, Sterl?' the man replied, rolling up an enormous joint and handing it over to Debbie for a draw before smoking it himself. He wasn't what Simon thought of as a Hell's Angel. For one thing, Skinner didn't have long hair, and for another, he wasn't wearing the distinctive denim waistcoat and emblems of a full-patch member. In fact, he didn't look like a Hell's Angel at all; more resembling a middle-aged plumber than any latter-day devotee of the infamous motorcycle gang that had had its origins way back in the 1960s.

'I need a gun, Jerry.'

'Whoa! Steady on kid. Tell me what happened first. There may be an easier way out of this.'

'There isn't.'

'What do you mean?'

'The girl — Tamara. I was *ordered* to rescue her.'

'Ordered? By whom?'

'By Cardinal de Valois, if you must know.'

'Shit—'

'Yeah, and that's not all.'

'Tell me.'

'The Vatican has declared a general cull of the undead and I'm *numero uno* on their hit list.'

'Oh… I see. That would explain the news then.'

'What news?'

'It was on the radio this morning. Three men killed in Vienna last night. They were decapitated apparently—'

Simon was out of his depth now. Part of him — the safe part — was thinking of edging his way slowly towards the door and making an exit from the room as fast as his legs would carry him. The other part — the detective part — was forcing him to sit exactly where he was and listen intently as the conversation between Sterling and Skinner unfolded. Quietly he watched as the woman in the mirrored sunglasses accepted the joint offered her by the grizzled old biker before slumping back into her armchair.

'I'm going to need that gun,' she said, taking a draw on the joint.

'Okay,' replied Skinner. 'I'll get in touch with Joe and see what he can lay his hands on.'

'No antiques, Jerry. I need a modern semi-automatic, tell him.'

'Shouldn't be a problem, Sterl. Give me a couple of days and I'll see what I can do.'

A couple of days, thought Simon. In the States, he could have just gone into a gun store and bought one off the shelf. Sterling turned her gaze towards him as if she'd read his mind. 'I'm sorry if you're feeling left out of things,' she said. 'All this must seem terribly strange to you.'

'You can say that again,' replied the detective. 'Who is Joe?'

'Joe is the leader of the biker gang that Jerry belongs to. They're based up in Harlow.'

'Where's that?'

'Essex. Not far.'

'And they can get you a gun?'

'Yeah, and just about anything else if you know how to ask.'

'I see... and they're Hell's Angels, right?'

'Yes. You got a problem with that?'

'No. We've got Angels over in the States. The HA are still pretty big in California. Always have been.'

'Joe still does some business with the Californians, but his main interests lie in the Netherlands these days. You know the sort of thing I mean...'

'Narcotics?'

'Mostly, but also a bit of money laundering on the side.'

'Sterling! He's a detective,' exclaimed Debbie, wide-eyed with astonishment. 'You shouldn't be saying those things in front of him.'

'Don't worry; he's sound,' put in Skinner, nodding at Simon as if to say, "You'd fucking well better be!" Sterling said nothing. She already knew.

'So, who's this Tamara woman?' piped up Debbie unscrewing the cap of the vodka bottle and pouring herself a drink. She offered the bottle to Simon who declined before replying: 'Tamara Sheridan is the daughter of an American multimillionaire called Randolph G. Sheridan. She was kidnapped outside a nightclub in Soho not so long ago.'

'Oh, yeah; I remember hearing something about it. Fotheringay's nightclub it was.'

'You know it?'

'Yeah. Right shit-hole it is. What the fuck was a high-end woman like her doing in a place like that?'

'Mind your language, Debbie,' put in Sterling with a grin. 'Mr Barrett is our guest here.'

'Sorry, Sterl. I was forgetting myself.'

'You always do, Debbs,' exclaimed Skinner taking a swig out of the bottle and handing it to Sterling. Then he took a draw from his joint and settled back in his chair. 'Fotheringay's is an alternative nightclub, Simon. It caters for all classes of people and is largely run by the underworld. In this respect, it is something of an anomaly in contemporary London with the exception of the Jabberwock Club up in Kilburn. Nightclubs are usually legitimate these days and the ones that aren't are usually fronts for money-laundering operations or otherwise immune from police investigation... if you get my drift.'

'The Mob?'

'Yes,' answered Sterling, 'or what passes for the Mob in England.'

'And what is your part in all of this might I ask?'

'My *part*, Simon?'

'Yeah. What do you get up to, you and your friends here? I mean, it's more than obvious to me that none of you exactly play by the rules.'

'I'm a grafter,' put in Debbie rescuing her vodka bottle from Sterling. 'I do shoplifting mostly and sell a bit of knock-off jewellery on the side. You know the sort of thing I mean — fake Rolexes, trainers, cosmetics and designer clothes; anything I can lay my hands on really. Skinner here has contacts with the Hell's Angels and their pharmaceutical interests, while Sterling acts as an enforcer, keeping the other London gangs in line. We're pretty big in the West End.'

'And the guy called the *cardinal* — what part does he play?'

'He's a member of the Catholic church, Mr Barrett,' answered Sterling. 'What else could he be?'

'But you said he ordered you to rescue Tamara. He sounds like an involved party.'

'It's complicated, Simon.'

'Oh... right. Can you elaborate on that?'

Skinner glanced at Sterling. 'It's okay, Jerry. I know what I'm doing,' she replied before turning back to the detective.

'You ever see a movie called *Twilight*, Simon?'

'Yes. I didn't think very much of it though.'

'Neither did I. In fact, I walked out of it halfway through laughing my tits off.'

'So, what are you trying to say, Sterling?'

Satisfied she had the detective's full attention, she leaned forward in her chair with both hands resting on her knees.

'Do you believe in vampires, Mr Barrett?'

'I don't disbelieve. I mean, I suppose there could be such a thing.'

'*Do- you- believe- in- vampires?*' Sterling repeated slowly, gazing directly into his eyes from behind her mirror shades.

Simon blinked, taken aback by the sudden change in Sterling's manner. 'If you mean, do I believe in the sort of vampires you see on TV, then no, I don't. Why do you ask?'

Sterling took off her sunglasses and looked at him, channelling her gaze directly into his mind. He remembered seeing two piercing orbs of crimson light where there should have been eyes, then fear took hold of him and he began trembling violently in his seat. Debbie looked away, hiding her face in her hands. She'd seen Sterling do this once before and didn't want to witness it again.

At first, he thought he was having an epileptic fit. There was a flash like an electric shock surging through his brain.

Then the room disappeared and Simon found himself in a very strange place:

The smell of blood and fear was strong. He knew he was witnessing everything Sterling had ever seen and done over a lifetime. He saw scenes of violence that would have shocked even the most hardened criminal, so intense were the images that now paraded before his mind's eye. In some, the hapless victims were seen trying to make a run for it before Sterling closed in for the kill. The screaming was the worst part, but it usually didn't last long before each individual was quickly despatched and drained of their blood with fiendish mechanical precision. Exactly what manner of creature he was dealing with, Simon did not know, but all these acts of carnage he was now witnessing certainly weren't the work of your average human killer. All he wanted to do now was tear himself away from Sterling's gaze and run. But he couldn't.

'Not yet, Mr Barrett!' came a voice out of the darkness. 'There's more…'

The scene now shifted to the interior of a fashionable London apartment where a party was in full swing. It was the year 1977 and a young woman with ginger hair dressed in the style of that period had just entered the room. Simon guessed the girl was called Julie Kent and that this would be the last time she was ever seen alive. The next series of images saw Julie as the victim of a frenzied vampire attack by a well known patrician lady called Virginia Cavendish, followed by an interval of time that culminated with Julie's body being washed up on a beach after Jimmy Silver had arranged to have it dumped somewhere out at sea. Several months passed in an instant, during which time Julie underwent her final metamorphosis into the creature that Simon now saw staring at him across the coffee table in Skinner's front room. The change was subtle at first, but when it was complete, there was no sign in those long, pale features and jet-black hair of Sterling's that Julie Kent had ever existed at all. As the days passed into years, Julie assumed the name of Sterling and developed an alarming drug habit. Now it was the 1980s and her desire for human blood and random acts of violence had increased to such an extent that she could no longer control it without taking enormous quantities of cocaine. By the late 1990s when by rights she should have been well into her forties, she had the fresh unblemished appearance of someone in their early twenties. She was now running a crime gang based in an old abandoned warehouse near Tower Bridge for their headquarters. Everything was going smoothly for them until one night Sterling and her associates descended on a mansion house in a remote part of rural Buckinghamshire and slaughtered everyone inside, including several members of the British establishment. This was too much for those who held power in the land and Sterling was forced to flee the country, travelling to Naples where she was gunned down in the street by two Camorra hitmen operating under the instructions of Jimmy Silver...*

'They use special bullets… You know what I'm saying?'

'They did what?' murmured Simon coming out of his trance.

'They used special bullets,' repeated Sterling, putting her sunglasses back on. 'The bullets were made of silver. Does that mean anything to you?'

The detective coughed and cleared his throat. 'Werewolves!' he declared. 'You need silver bullets to kill werewolves!'

'Good,' said Sterling; 'you're getting warmer. Anything else?'

Simon shook his head failing to make the connection, at which point Sterling decided to force the issue:

'Do you remember me telling you that Jimmy Silver used to be called Sir James Blackthorne back in the eighteenth century…?'

'Yes, I do. I presumed you were having a joke.'

'Well I wasn't. Why do you think I was born in 1977 as Julie Kent but only look twenty years of age?'

'You've had plastic surgery?'

Sterling shook her head.

'Good genes?'

'Quite the opposite, Mr Barrett. There's nothing good about my genes or Jimmy Silver's for that matter.'

'I'm still not following you.'

'Okay, let me put it another way. What is it that myself and Jimmy Silver have in common?'

'You both look a whole lot younger than you should be.'

'Correct. And why is that, Simon?'

'I don't rightly know. Are you both related or something?'

'Yes, in a manner of speaking, we are.'

'But how? You told me that Silver was born in the eighteenth century…'

'Indeed I did.'

'Then how are you related? I don't get it?'

Sterling lowered her head in despair. Then she raised her gaze once more and answered him:

'Because we're both vampires, Simon! There, I trust that answers you question. Now let's go and find Tamara.'

8

'Wouldn't it be better to go back to Tamara's flat?' exclaimed Simon, not at all certain why they were both standing in the central chamber of a dilapidated Victorian warehouse somewhere near the river Thames.

The vampire wasn't listening. She was too busy rummaging her way through a large pile of books and magazines to take any notice. That the old warehouse was somehow where she lived was obvious to Simon, both by her familiarity with the building and by the way she'd casually flung her leather jacket onto a nearby chair when they'd first entered the room.

'Where's that fucking book?' she snarled. 'I know I put it down here somewhere but I can't seem to find it.'

'What book is that, Sterling?'

'The book Cardinal de Valois gave me. It was some sort of grimoire.'

'What's a *grimoire?*'

'A handbook of ritual magic if you must know. Here, Simon, make yourself useful and help me look for it. It's a small, leather-bound book about the size of a pocket diary.'

'This it?' the detective replied, picking up a brown rectangular object from the floor and handing it to Sterling.

'Ah-ha!' she exclaimed, snatching the slim volume from Simon's outstretched hand and thumbing her way through its pages with ferocious speed, all the while muttering to herself as she did so.

'What's a senior member of the Catholic church doing dabbling in magic for?' enquired Simon. 'I thought they were dead against that sort of thing.'

'Not when they deem it necessary, Mr Barrett. In any case, Cardinal de Valois isn't just a member of the Catholic church. He's also an Adept.'

'What's one of them?'

'You don't want to know and I can't tell you. It's bad for your health, if you get my meaning.'

The detective sat down on a chair. The hour was getting late. It had been some time since they'd been in Skinner's flat in Islington and now he was alone with the strange woman again in a place that seemed to function as her home. Gazing around, his attention was drawn to the furniture in the room. Some of it was clearly centuries old and covered in a thick layer of dust. Was the woman really what she claimed to be or had the antique furniture already been in the warehouse when she'd moved in?

'It was the year 1977, Mr Barrett,' Sterling remarked, glancing up from her book. 'That was when my life as Julie Kent ended and I became the thing I am now. I trust that satisfies your curiosity.'

'You came here in 1977?'

'Not quite, Simon. It happened a bit later than that, but you can check out my history in all those old newspaper cuttings and magazines over there on the sofa if you like. They date back to 1977. It's the year I went missing.'

The detective got up from his chair and walked over to the sofa. Picking up one of the yellowed newspaper cuttings, he began reading:

'"... *Julie Kent, daughter of Albert and Molly Kent, went missing at the Roxy Nightclub in July 1977...*" Well, yes, there is a faint resemblance to you in the press photograph I'll admit, but this newspaper article is well over forty years old. How come you look so young?'

'Because vampires don't age, Simon,' she smiled. 'Every third-grader knows that. It's in all the B-movies ever made.'

He hated it when she smiled. There was nothing remotely human in that smile. In fact, it was the very absence of humanity that he disliked the most. Something cold and hard that chilled him to the bone.

'I still don't believe you,' he said, sitting down once more. 'There's no such thing.'

Sterling didn't answer him. Her attention had been caught by the sound of a motorcycle engine in the street outside. 'That must be Joe,' she exclaimed. 'I'd better let him in.'

'I came as fast as I could, Sterl. The traffic was a bit thick on account of some roadworks south of Harlow.'

Joe Rackham was more the image of a Hell's Angel than Jerry Skinner had been. His hair was longer for a start and he was wearing the famous HA emblem on the back of his motorcycle jacket. Noting Simon as he walked in through the door, he nodded his head in his direction.

'Who's this, Sterling? You didn't say there was going to be anyone else here.'

'His name is Simon Barrett, Joe. He's a detective.'

'He's a *what*—?'

'It's okay. Everything's cool. Mr Barrett is a private investigator, not a real copper. He's over here from America on business.'

'What kind of business?'

'I'm investigating the disappearance and possible kidnapping of an American citizen,' put in Simon getting up from the sofa and squaring up to the biker. Instinct told him not to offer a handshake.

'Is he on the level?' enquired Joe looking at Sterling.

'He's sound,' the vampire replied. 'Would you like a coffee or maybe something a bit stronger?'

'Just coffee for me thanks,' replied the biker seating himself down on a chair in front of a low, rectangular table. Simon mirrored his move and sat back down on the sofa. Joe lit up a Marlboro and offered him one from the packet.

'No thanks,' said Simon. 'I used to smoke but I gave them up.'

'Very wise,' murmured Joe in a thick Essex accent. 'So, who's this American citizen you're looking for?'

'Her name is Tamara Sheridan,' ventured Simon. 'You heard of her?'

Joe pondered for a moment. 'Nah, can't say that I have, but I'll let you know if I hear anything. People in my line of business sometimes get to know stuff. Ain't that right Sterling?'

'You what, Joe?' came a voice from the interior of what passed for a kitchen in the building.

'I said, I would tell the detective here if I heard anything about the Tamara Sheridan woman.'

'Oh, right — and you can tell me as well,' replied the vampire, returning from the kitchen with two steaming mugs of coffee. 'I've got Cardinal de Valois and half the Vatican breathing down my neck wanting her found at all costs.'

'I know. Skinner told me you were having a few

problems.'

'And did he tell you about the cull as well?'

'Yes. It's the main reason why I'm here,' replied Joe removing a small manila parcel from the inside pocket of his jacket and sliding it across the table towards Sterling. 'It's a Walther 9mm semi-automatic pistol with a full magazine.'

'Is it clean?'

'About as clean as I am. Take it or leave it, Sterl. It's all I could get.'

'How much?'

'It's on the house, Sterling. I owe you.'

Sterling unwrapped the parcel and took out the gun, playing it through her fingers.

'Hey, watch where you're pointing that thing!' exclaimed Simon shielding his face with his hands.

'It's okay mate. She knows what she's doing. In any case, the safety catch is on. I checked the gun before I left Harlow. Didn't want the fucker going off in me pocket on the way down, did I?'

'It feels good, Joe,' put in Sterling. 'I'll take it.'

Joe nodded and sat back in his chair. 'This place hasn't changed much,' he remarked glancing around the room. 'Last time I was here, we had the whole crew down from Essex planning that hit on Jimmy Silver.'

'That's what I was about to tell you, Joe.'

'What were you about to tell me?'

'The girl — Tamara…'

'What about her?'

'Silver was involved in her kidnapping. De Valois wants her found at all costs.'

Joe sat forward in his chair with a look of concern. 'Silver, you say? I thought we put him out of action a couple of years ago.'

'We did, but we didn't kill him, Joe. He managed to escape — remember?'

'How can I forget? I almost lost half my team when we entered that spooky old house of his. You know — the one you torched with the holy water.'

'Yeah. It was nearly on top for the lot of us that night, Joe. I didn't think he'd be back so soon but it looks like he's up to his old tricks again.'

'Just what is it with you and Jimmy Silver, Sterl? Why the constant vendetta?'

'It's a long story, Joe. Ask Skinner about it the next time you see him. He'll fill you in on all the details.'

'No. I want to hear it from you.'

The vampire stopped playing with the gun and laid it down on the table opposite to where Simon was seated. Almost tempted to pick it up, the detective thought better of it and reached for his coffee instead, only too aware that he was being closely watched by Joe who was by now more than halfway through his third Marlboro and showing no signs of flagging.

'Okay, Joe,' said Sterling flopping down into a chair. 'Silver and me have been at one another's throats for years. The feud goes back a long way.'

'How far?'

The vampire grinned. 'Back to the nineteen seventies, Joe. That's when I first joined the ranks of the undead. Silver had been around for centuries and I was the new kid on the block. He saw something in me he didn't like.'

'Such as what?'

'Such as the fact that I'm just as powerful as he is and then some. Only thing is, he's had a head start on me by about two hundred years, which kind of gives him the upper hand in most things.'

'Yeah, Skinner mentioned something about that. Jimmy's managed to extend his criminal activities across most of Europe, I understand. He's a regular *Moriarty* by all accounts.'

'Yes, Joe; and I'm his nemesis. He knows there's going to be a final showdown one of these days and he wants to be prepared for it when it comes.'

'That what you want the gun for then?'

'No. It's just for protection.'

'And the American woman — what's her part in all of this?'

Simon could tell the biker was no fool. Already well into his fifties, Joe was as street-savvy as they came, and probably a good deal more sophisticated than he looked. Sterling balked at his question.

'Tamara is Silver's secret weapon, Joe. According to what de Valois said, Jimmy plans to use her as his brood mare.'

'His what…?'

'He plans to sire a child with her. It's his way of ensuring he has a successor to his criminal empire if things go badly for him.'

'I don't get it, Sterl. Why would he want to do that?'

'Out of spite, Joe. He knows that if things go tits up for him, then it's only a question of time before his position in the undead hierarchy is usurped by someone younger. There aren't that many contenders for his throne, but I'm one of them.'

'But you're one of his offspring.'

'Yes, I guess I am, but he still doesn't like me. I'm a child of the 1970s, remember. We don't play by the rules. Silver represents the old world — the world of dukes, lords and kings. He's well over two hundred years old for fuck's sake — what do you expect?'

'So, what are you saying, Sterling? Are you telling me that vampires have a class system all of their own?'

'The older ones do. A few of them even have titles and property dating back to the time when they were still part of the nobility.'

Simon raised his eyebrows. He still didn't believe the charade being played out in front of him, but the idea that vampires might actually possess a class system he found mildly amusing. 'You told me that you used to be called Julie Kent, Sterling,' he said interrupting her. 'Is the name, Sterling your alias then?'

The vampire glanced at Joe then regarded the detective in the same way that an irate parent might glower at a fractious child. 'No, Simon,' she said quietly. 'The name Sterling was one I adopted back in the seventies. I used to be involved with the Punk movement back then and it was fashionable to adopt a pseudonym if you wanted to impress your friends. It's kind of stuck with me ever since for the simple reason that I do not remember being Julie Kent. It's what happens when you become one of the undead. Your former life as a mortal is erased… along with your soul. I trust that answers your question, detective?'

Her answer was so matter-of-fact, Simon almost found himself believing it. Looking at Joe for signs of mirth, he found none. Just the same cold hard stare gazing out at him from a granite face. Evidently, Joe was party to whatever it was that was going on between Sterling and Skinner. Maybe they all worked as a team, including the young blonde woman called Debbie. Perhaps she was in on the joke, as well?

'Anyway, thanks for the gun, Joe,' exclaimed Sterling pocketing the weapon. 'All I need now is a good night's sleep and some herbs in the morning.'

'On the weed, Sterl? I thought you only did coke as a rule.'

'They're not the kind of herbs you're thinking of, Joe. It's just some stuff I need so I can perform a bit of ritual magic, that's all'

'Your usual supplier then?'

'Yeah. I'll get them from that shop up near the British Museum. They've usually got what I require.'

'Okay. Well, if there's nothing else you need, I'll be on my way. It's a long drive back up to Harlow so I'd best be off.'

'Thanks… Oh, and Joe—'

'Yes?'

'You haven't got much else on at the moment I hope?'

'No, I haven't Sterling. Why do you ask?'

'Just a thought. I might need some help over the next few days, that's all. I don't think Silver's going to give Tamara up without making a fight of it.'

9

'This is the place,' exclaimed Sterling, standing outside the shop. *"Irene's Potions and Curiosities,"* the oldest occult supplier in London. You can get anything you want here.'

'Yeah, I bet,' muttered Simon to himself as he gazed in the window. It was filled with all manner of arcane paraphernalia, including a shop-window mannequin of a scantily clad young woman wearing a domino mask and very little else who was clearly engaged in some kind of magical ceremony set against the painted backdrop of a night sky with a full moon.

'What's all this about?' queried the detective.

'She's meant to be a witch, Mr Barrett. Quite a senior one by the look of that mask she's wearing. Don't worry — it's only a showroom dummy.'

'I wasn't worrying — just curious, that's all. We get this sort of thing in the States but only in New Orleans and places like that. The Christian fundamentalists are always trying to close them down. Which reminds me; I need to investigate that evangelical organisation that Tamara belonged to.'

'Later, Simon. We need to attend to darker matters for now.'

TING! An old-fashioned bell above the door announced their presence as they entered the shop. Inside, it was surprisingly modern and well lit. All around the walls, arranged by subject rather than author's name, were a dazzling array of books dealing with every magical subject imaginable.

"*Practical Spell-Casting for Beginners?*" exclaimed the detective, pulling out one of the volumes and thumbing his way through the first dozen pages or so.

'Over here, Simon—' hissed Sterling walking towards the counter. 'We haven't come to browse.'

'Can I help you?' said the demure-looking young lady standing behind the till. She had chocolate-brown hair and was dressed in the latest 1950s retro-chic, complete with a pair of horn-rimmed spectacles perched on the end of her nose.

'She doesn't look much like a witch to me,' whispered Simon to Sterling as they approached the counter.

'That's because she's not. She's actually a well-known Sensitive.'

'A what?'

'She's a psychic. It's probably why she works here. Places like this function as safe havens for people of her kind.'

'Uh... okay, Sterling. You're the expert.'

Simon was none the wiser for this revelation and decided to let his companion do all the talking.

'I'd like to purchase a few things if I may,' said Sterling to the young woman behind the counter.

'Sure. What do you need?'

The woman's jaw dropped as the vampire reeled off her list of items: 'Henbane, hemlock, saffron powder, cloves, mandrake root, opium, four black candles and some rue please.'

'We don't have opium,' the woman replied. 'Can't get a licence for it.'

'Okay, I'll have to use some charlie instead,' exclaimed Sterling with a smile. 'Have you got the rest?'

The woman nodded. 'Just a moment. We keep most of our

stock in the back shop. I won't be long'

'What do you want with all of that?' exclaimed Simon as he watched the woman disappear into the back room.

'It's the stuff we'll need for when we perform the spell.'

'What spell?'

'You'll see. Just meet me outside Highgate Cemetery at around midnight tonight and I'll explain everything.'

'I don't understand...'

'You don't have to, Simon. Just remember to bring a torch, a one-gallon can full of petrol and a slot-headed screwdriver with you when you come. I'll do the rest.'

***

Simon spent most of the day in his hotel room making occasional forays into the street to purchase a coffee and something to eat. Once or twice he thought of contacting Tamara's father to inform him of his progress in finding his daughter, but thought better of it when it dawned on him that he'd actually achieved nothing so far in the way of tracking down the girl other than visiting an occult bookshop with someone who claimed to be a vampire and who was adamant that she could find out where Tamara was.

Matters weren't helped when around about two o'clock in the afternoon there was a knock on his door. It was one of the hotel cleaners requesting access to his room so she could spruce it up a bit and change the bed. Like the polite fool he was, Simon obliged her by vacating his room for an interval so she could do whatever it was she was required to do. When he returned, he found a sealed envelope placed strategically on his pillow with his name on it. Of the chambermaid there was no sign.

Reaching down, he picked up the envelope. It was secured with an old-fashioned wax seal which broke in two when he opened it. Inside the envelope was a letter written in purple ink on pale blue paper scented with cologne. The penmanship was exquisite but the message proved otherwise:

Dear Mr Barrett

Please forgive the manner in which this letter was delivered. I have attempted to contact you through various of my menials, but on all occasions you have proved elusive to the point of distraction. Be that as it may, it has been drawn to my attention that you have been making enquiries into the whereabouts of a certain Miss Tamara Sheridan, daughter of Randolph G. Sheridan, resident of the city of New York. It has also been reported that you have lately come into the confidence of a certain woman who goes by the name of Sterling and who claims, not without some degree of truth, to be a Vampire. Might I suggest that you desist from your current line of investigation and remove yourself from the company of this woman, not only for the sake of your health, but also to preserve your own mental stability and equilibrium. Return to your native land as soon as possible and without delay, for I fear that if you do not, the consequences both for yourself and for all those who you hold dear may prove grave.

Your obedient servant
James Silver

Running to the door, Simon glanced up and down the corridor hoping to catch a glimpse of the chambermaid, but there was no sign of her. She was gone, along with her trolley and vacuum cleaner, either to some other floor of the hotel or out of the building altogether, never having been a real chambermaid in the first place. Muttering an oath, he returned to his room and re-read the letter. That it was a veiled threat was obvious to him, but what had been the motive of its sender?

James Silver... wasn't that the guy Sterling had mentioned? His handwriting was archaic to the point of absurdity, and the envelope had been sealed with a monogrammed red wax seal; something that hadn't been in fashion for well over a century or more. Just the sort of thing an elderly vampire would do. But real vampires didn't exist, did they? It just wasn't possible. Someone was trying to scare him off. Either that or everything he had encountered so far was nothing more than an elaborate hoax designed to put him off the scent and send him scurrying off back to America empty-handed. Well, whoever was behind it, they would find him a tougher nut to crack than they bargained for. He owed it to Randolph Sheridan and he owed it to Tamara, wherever she was. Maybe his visit to Highgate Cemetery with Sterling might shed a bit of light on the matter. If it didn't, then he would abandon the crazy bitch and strike out on his own. He had at least another month to spend in the UK and almost unlimited resources to tide him over. Something was bound to turn up, eventually.

10

There was a storm brewing by the time Simon reached the cemetery. The wind had been picking up for most of the afternoon and by late evening it was of sufficient strength to send the crisp autumn leaves scurrying madly across the pavement in front of him.

So this was London's famous Highgate Cemetery. But where was Sterling, he wondered, as he checked the contents of his carrier bag — a one-gallon container full of petrol, a cheap, battery-powered torch and a slot-headed screwdriver just like she'd said. The torch he could understand. They would need that to find their way through the cemetery at night. But the petrol — what the hell was that for?

Ten minutes to midnight and she still hadn't arrived. Listening in vain for the sound of a motorcycle engine, Simon paced the tarmac in front of the cemetery gates wishing for all the world that he was back in his warm hotel bedroom sipping neat bourbon whiskey in front of the television. Overhead, ragged clouds were racing across the moon, accompanied by the occasional rumble of thunder coming from somewhere over to the west. Another instant and the heavens opened up with a crackle of lightning loud enough to wake the dead. For some reason Simon turned and found himself staring straight into the black, mirrored sunglasses of his friend.

'You!'

Sterling looked different this time. The sunglasses were

the same, but she was wearing her hair tied back in a ponytail and carried a brown leather satchel slung on a strap across one shoulder.

'Did you bring the petrol and screwdriver like I told you?' she said glancing down at Simon's carrier bag.

'Yes, I did,' replied the detective looking around to check if they were being observed. 'What do you need them for?'

'You'll see. Just follow me and all with be revealed.'

It wasn't very wide. The gap in the wall behind the hanging ivy was just big enough to allow for the passage of a slim adult providing they entered it sideways. Once they were through, Simon switched on his torch. 'What now?' he said peering into the forested gloom.

'This is the Western Cemetery,' Sterling replied. 'It's the oldest part of Highgate.'

'So?'

Sterling beckoned him along the path. 'Because it's where Marie Gibeau is buried,' she replied, leading the way down an overgrown lane that was lined with trees and ancient gravestones on either side.

'Who is Marie Gibeau?' asked the detective, not at all sure if he knew where he was going.

'Marie Gibeau was a nineteenth-century voodoo priestess from Haiti. She lived in London for a time during the Victorian era. At least, that's what I was told.'

'Told by whom?'

'Cardinal de Valois. He's something of an expert in these matters.'

'What's a Catholic priest doing messing around with voodoo?'

'How should I know? Comes with the job I suppose. He

also knows I'm a vampire for what it's worth. Come, let's go.'

'Where to?'

'The tomb of Marie Gibeau of course. Where do you think?'

Another few minutes of threading his way through the twisting pathways and dense undergrowth of the cemetery and Simon found himself standing at the entrance of what looked to all the world like a street of small houses heavily festooned with ivy and richly ornate funeral sculpture.

'What is this place?' he said, playing the beam of his torch along the gently curving avenue of stone buildings.

'It's a necropolis, Simon. Each one of these little houses is a mausoleum where the wealthy inhabitants of Victorian London used to bury their dead. Marie's tomb is around here somewhere. At least that's what this guide book says.'

Simon shone his torch over the pamphlet Sterling was holding in her hand. 'Oh, yeah, so it is,' he remarked casually. 'What are we going to do when we find it?'

'Do, Simon? We're going to break into it, that's what we're going to do, and then we're going to have ourselves a little chat with Marie if that's all right with you. She's going to tell us where Tamara is and maybe Jimmy Silver as well if we're lucky. Now, come along. Follow me. We haven't got much time.'

Silently, they crept towards the stone vaults, carefully checking each one in turn. Some were unmarked and sadly neglected, either without their iron doors or overgrown with high bushes and saplings. Others were perfectly preserved, almost as if they had recently been built or at least scrupulously maintained by the descendants of those interred within. Simon was just about to say something when he saw the tent.

It was a sort of fairground tent, with a sloped roof and high, steep sides flowing down from neatly scalloped eaves. He thought for a moment that he had stumbled upon a party of campers or a workman's shelter set between two of the more classical vaults in the row. But the tent was made of stone. It was white granite or marble, with carved folds, and it bore an inscription on the lintel above the door: *"Marie Gibeau, Fortune Teller & Clairvoyant; 1825 – 1879."*

'That must have been how she earned her living,' said Sterling regarding the chiselled inscription. 'Quite a mean poker player too by all accounts.'

Simon stepped closer and examined the door of the mausoleum with his flashlight. It was made of metal and secured by a strong brass padlock on a rusty hasp. 'Here,' said Sterling, 'let me try.'

Reaching into her pocket, she took out a long thin key and began waggling it around in the lock. 'Something I borrowed from Debbie,' she remarked. 'It's a skeleton key. One of the best.'

A few moments later and a soft, metallic click told Simon that the lock was free. Pulling the hasp aside, Sterling pushed on the heavy iron door which groaned on its hinges as it opened. Then the detective gasped in astonishment. He was looking directly into the chamber of a tomb.

In the icy beam of his torch, the tomb looked very murky and not at all like its magnificent exterior. It was a terrible little room, dusty and unkempt with the coffin lying on the floor at an acute angle to the walls. Evidently, whoever had placed it there all those years ago hadn't been too bothered by ceremony. A solitary wreath of dried flowers lay on top of the coffin, the petals long since crumbled into dust.

'Good,' declared Sterling. 'The lid is still intact. That means it hasn't been tampered with. Hand me the screwdriver, Simon.'

'Why — what are you going to do?'

'Open it up, that's what.'

'But you can't do that! It's desecration!'

She wasn't listening. One by one, the rusted screws yielded to her awesome strength. When they were all out, she looked up at the detective.

'Are you ready for this, Simon?'

'Ready for what?'

'Lifting the coffin lid of course. Come on, give me a hand. This thing looks a bit awkward.'

He'd never seen a corpse before. At least not one that had been lying in its grave for over a hundred years. Reputed to have been a handsome woman in her time, Marie Gibeau lay in her coffin with her withered, stick-like arms crossed over her chest and her strong mulatto features shrunken into her skull in the manner of an ancient Egyptian mummy. What looked like a deck of playing cards had been placed beneath her bony fingers; presumably a parting gift from some friend or lover when she'd been interred. Other than that, there was nothing else in the casket apart from a small bottle of Jamaican rum set on the faded, satin pillow which supported her head.

'Sterling, why are we doing this?'

'Because we're going to perform a spell, Simon. Why do you think I went to that shop this morning to buy all those things? They're what we need to summon the goddess Hecate.'

'Who?'

'Hecate. She's the deity who guards the world of the dead.'

'But why should we want to do that?'

'So we can talk to Marie, silly. Why do you think?'

'What do you mean talk to her? She's been a freakin' corpse for over a hundred years for Christ's sake!'

'Not for very much longer, detective. Here, help me lift her out of the coffin and lay her on the floor.'

Reluctantly, Simon took hold of the grisly cadaver. It was emaciated and stiff, the skin having the consistency of desiccated parchment. Placing the body on the floor with its head facing east, Simon took a step back. 'What do we do now?' he said, wiping his hands on the lapels of his coat before picking up his flashlight.

'Now we perform the ritual of the dead,' Sterling replied rummaging around in her satchel and laying its contents out on a small octagonal table that formed the only item of furniture in the room. 'These are the offerings to the goddess Hecate. We can use this table for our altar…'

The detective didn't reply. He was standing at the door of the mausoleum squinting out into the darkness.

'Simon, what are you doing over there?'

'I think I heard a noise in the bushes,' he replied turning round. 'It's probably nothing — just some animal or other.'

'Fine. If it's okay, then there's nothing to worry about. Come back inside. I'm going to light these four black candles and begin the ritual. You can watch if you like.'

Simon looked on as his companion walked solemnly around the corpse in a clockwise direction reciting some words from the book she was holding in her hand. One by one, she lit the four black candles then stood beside the corpse in the middle of the circle she'd drawn on the floor with a piece of chalk. 'Step inside the circle, Simon,' she commanded, pouring some foul-smelling liquid out of a glass vial into a small circular dish she'd placed beside the corpse.

'No, I'd rather not if that's all right with you.'

'Step inside the circle. It's for your own protection. Do it now!'

Her voice sounded dark and hollow as if it came from another world, and the detective felt himself compelled to step over the chalk line and into the circle until he was standing close beside her next to the makeshift altar and the foul-smelling dish of liquid.

Smearing her hands with henna, Sterling clicked her cigarette lighter and set fire to the contents of the dish. Soon, the smell grew stronger as a thick column of smoke began spiralling upward towards the ceiling of the mausoleum. Then she began:

Throwing back her head and with both hands raised, Sterling let out a long howl like that of a wolf. If Simon could have laughed, he would have done so, but for some reason the laughter never came. Instead, he just stood rooted to the spot, realising in his heart of hearts that somehow this ceremony was the real thing and that his neat and tidy view of the universe was about to be shattered forever.

A crash of thunder rolled across the sky, followed by a burst of lightning so intense that it penetrated the darkest recesses of the room. This had the effect of spotlighting the corpse on the floor in such a way that it gave it the appearance of life. At least, that was how it seemed from where Simon was standing, inside the circle with Sterling who by now had ceased her canine howling and was swaying gently from side to side in a light trance.

Then she began to speak. Slowly at first and with great authority, she addressed the corpse on the floor with the words; 'By virtue of the goddess Hecate and the agonies of the damned, I conjure and command thee, spirit of Marie Gibeau deceased, to answer all my questions and demands, on pain of everlasting torment. Berald, Beroald, Balbin, Gab, Gabor, Agaba, arise, arise I charge and command thee!'

Outside, the sound of thunder grew in intensity until it began to echo from the walls of the dimly lit chamber, causing the very stones of which it was made to vibrate in unison with the storm. Another burst of lightning flickered through the open doorway and across the floor, illuminating the corpse of Marie Gibeau in its ghostly glare.

Looking on with a mixture of horror and fascination, the detective watched as Marie's body took on the appearance of someone who was not long dead but merely sleeping. Her flesh was visibly thickening in front of his eyes and her skin had taken on a warm glow suggestive of life.

Unclean... That was the word that formed in Simon's mind as he observed the body slowly rise up, unsupported from the floor and hover vertically in a standing position barely a few inches away from his face. Something terribly unclean was taking place here and he wanted no part of it. In a panic, he made to run from the circle and out into the night, but Sterling grabbed him by the arm.

'No! Stay where you are, Simon. To leave the circle now will mean certain death for you. We are both closer to Hell in this room than you could ever begin to imagine. Stay with me and all will be well. Leave and you are surely damned.'

Her words had a soothing effect, causing him to relax a

little even though he was still gazing directly into the face of a living corpse. It was strange, he thought, how Marie just hung there in mid-air with only one toe anchoring her to the ground. Stranger still was the way the walls of the room had begun to shimmer and dissolve away into inky blackness as if they had never exited at all.

'We are in the abode of the dead, Simon. The goddess, Hecate has granted us access to the spirit world. Why don't you ask Marie a question.'

'Such as what?'

'You already know what. Just ask her the question and she will answer it one way or another. It's not as if she's got any choice in the matter.'

The detective braced himself and swallowed hard before addressing the hovering ghoul: 'Spirit of Marie Gibeau, be so good as to tell us where Tamara Sheridan, daughter of Randolph George Sheridan may be found, for we fear she may be in mortal danger of her life.'

There was no response from the floating spectre. Outside, the sound of thunder seemed distant and remote as if it were far away in some other dimension. Nothing moved in the death chamber apart from the steady flame of the four black candles set around the chalk circle on the floor. The silence was palpable.

'Try again,' hissed Sterling, 'and this time, make sure you *demand* an answer.'

'Okay, I'll try,' replied the detective thinking fast. 'Perhaps this might work: Hey, Marie; you wanna play some poker?'

The corpse twitched and opened its eyes. A thin smile fluttered across its lips.

'Nice one, Simon,' muttered his companion. 'Now ask her the frigging question.'

'Right then, here goes... Uh, spirit of Marie Gibeau, I command you to reveal the whereabouts of Tamara Sheridan on pain of everlasting torment...'

The dry lips of the revenant began to open, trying to form words it hadn't used in years, but nothing came out of its mouth apart from a few empty grunts and vowel sounds.

'What's up?' said Simon. 'Why won't she speak?'

'Because she's been dead for well over a hundred years. How would you feel if you hadn't spoken for over a century or more? Give her some time for fuck's sake.'

For what seemed like an age, they watched and waited as the living corpse struggled to speak. At length, the words began to make some kind of sense, eventually running into whole phrases and scattered sentences: 'The girl... Tamara... she will not be found anywhere within these shores. She is being held far away in a distant land... shielded by powerful magic... in a dark place... underground.'

'How can we find her?' put in Sterling, growing agitated. Simon too was becoming increasingly concerned by this revelation.

'She was taken by way of Holland,' Marie continued. 'She was taken to the city of Amsterdam and the Angels received her there. More than that, I cannot say. Her trail has grown cold... even for those with the vision of the Dead.'

Sterling nodded her head sagely. 'Hmm, Angels you say. And did these *angels* happen to ride on motorcycles by any chance?'

'They had machines, yes.'

'What's she saying, Sterling?' interrupted Simon. 'What's

all this about angels? Is it because Tamara is dead or something?'

'No, Simon. It's got nothing to do with that.'

'Then what?'

Sterling gave a wry smile: 'Oh, let's just say that I'm going to have a quiet word with Skinner and Joe when we're finished here. I think they've got a bit of explaining to do.'

'I don't understand. What about?'

'People trafficking, that's what! Now, let's put Marie back into her box and get the fuck out of here. Stand aside while I perform the closing ritual then hand me that can of petrol.'

'Why — what are you going to do?'

'Cremate the body, Simon. What else?'

'But you can't do that!'

'Watch me—'

***

'Was that really necessary?' queried Simon as they made their way back down the cemetery path.

'Yes,' replied Sterling turning her head to look round. Behind them, a lurid orange glow could already be seen emerging from the doorway of the mausoleum as the fire quickly consumed Marie's corpse. 'Once a spirit has been summoned from the dead, the only way it can be returned to whence it came is if the body is cremated.'

'Are you sure of that?'

'Well, that's what it says in this book, Cardinal de Valois gave me, so I guess it must be true.'

They walked on, not quite certain if they were heading in the right direction. Up ahead, something caught Simon's eye.

The light of his torch was already beginning to dim, but he could just about make out a grey shape moving among the tombstones. 'There's someone here,' he said halting in his stride.

'I've seen him,' acknowledged Sterling pretending not to notice.

'Who do you think it is?'

'I don't know, but I've got my suspicions. Just keep on walking, Simon.'

They both carried on as if nothing had happened, moving further down the path until they came to a junction where a statue of an angel with its wings outstretched stood atop of a large marble plinth, no doubt marking the tomb of some long-dead Victorian worthy.

'He's over there by the laurel bushes,' Sterling whispered, reaching inside her satchel.

'Where? I can't see him.'

The words were scarcely out of Simon's mouth when something shiny and metallic whistled through the air between himself and where his friend was standing a couple of metres to his right.

'He's using a crossbow.'

'He's what?'

'He's got a crossbow, Simon. Keep your head down.'

Without further prompting, the detective crouched down behind the marble plinth hardly daring to breathe.

'Why is he shooting at us, Sterling?'

'Don't worry, Simon. It's me he's trying to hit, not you.'

'But why?'

'Can't you guess?' the vampire replied pulling something out of her satchel. 'This gun Joe got me should settle the fucker's hash.'

'Sterling, you can't be serious—'

Blam! Blam! Blam! Blam!

For a couple of seconds, nothing happened and then a body fell out of the bushes onto the path, a crossbow clattering down beside it. All around was stillness, the thunderstorm having long since passed over leaving the sky clear and bright with stars. Simon switched off his torch to save the battery; then he walked over to the body with Sterling.

'It's a Catholic priest!' he exclaimed in surprise looking down at the bullet-riddled corpse.

'He's a Church of England vicar to be precise,' replied Sterling examining the body. 'He must have been drafted in by the Vatican to help out with the cull.'

'You mean the vampire cull?'

'Yes. Catholic priests are a bit thin on the ground in England so the Vatican must have joined forces with the Anglican Church for the duration. Here, give me a hand turning him over.'

With one hand under the dead man's shoulder, Simon turned the body and watched as Sterling searched through his pockets, taking out what looked like a small, black leather wallet.

'Ah, ha! That's what I was looking for,' she declared, opening the wallet.

'What is it, Sterling?'

'His calling card, Simon, that's what. He's a member of the Order of Exorcists just as I expected.'

Removing a slim plastic card from the wallet, she handed it to Simon who read it carefully under the beam of his torch. His friend was right. The guy was a trained exorcist with all the right credentials, including a Masters degree in theology.

'He's packing too,' Sterling added, pulling the lapel of the man's coat aside.

'What — you mean he's got a gun?'

'No, stupid. There are two silver crossbow bolts hidden in a secret holster beneath his jacket. Look…'

Simon looked. Sure enough, the flights of two small arrows were protruding from a compact leather holster secured by a strap around the priest's torso. There was space for a third but it was missing, presumably having recently been fired.

'These were meant for me, Simon. Two silver crossbow bolts carried by a priest. Now do you know what I am?'

'Er, no I don't Sterling.'

'Christ all fucking mighty, just what does it take with you?'

'I… I…'

'Turn your back, Simon.'

'What?'

'Turn your back. Do it now!'

The detective turned away. All he could hear was a steady sucking and gurgling sound coming from where Sterling was crouched down low over the body of the priest. When the noise stopped, he turned to look but wished he hadn't.

'Welcome to my world, Mr Barrett,' was all she said staring up at him with her lips engorged with fresh blood. 'Welcome to my world.'

11

Simon had never met a cardinal before.

He'd been to a party in Boston where everyone had to come dressed as a member of the clergy, but he'd never actually seen the real thing.

On the surface, Cardinal de Valois looked like anyone else of a certain age. Hair greying at the temples but with some remnant of colour at the crown, the man seemed to be hovering somewhere between his late fifties and early sixties, give or take a few years or so. Only the eyes suggested the presence of a far younger and more agile mind.

He was as usual on these more intimate occasions, not wearing his full regalia, but instead remained seated in his wing-back chair clad only in a plain black cassock with a short, shoulder-length tunic trimmed with purple satin and a cherry red skull-cap perched on the back of his head.

The cardinal took up a medium-sized brandy glass and swirled its contents gently beneath his nose for a moment before raising it, saying:

'It was careless of you to lose Tamara like that.'

'For what it's worth, Edward,' exclaimed Sterling angrily, 'I nearly got myself killed out there in the cemetery last night.'

She'd been holding it back for the better part of ten minutes ever since they'd entered the room, but now her rage had surfaced in a tirade of expletives directed at just about every organised religion on the planet.

'—and another thing. Since when has the Church of England thought of extending its sphere of activities to vampire hunting?'

'You'll have to take that one up with Lambeth Palace, my dear. As you know, my orders come directly from the Vatican.'

'Not funny, Edward. The cunt had a crossbow as well!'

'I'm sorry, Sterling. I honestly don't know what that vicar was doing there. The vampire cull is strictly a papal matter, or so I was led to believe.'

'Thanks a bunch,' she replied, slumping down into an adjacent chair like a teenage schoolgirl in a huff. 'So, now we've got another mystery on our hands.'

Simon lifted the glass of whisky he'd been toying with. 'What if the vicar was working for Jimmy Silver?'

De Valois raised an eyebrow. 'Your friend has a point, Sterling. What if the man was one of Silver's agents or someone in the Church he'd managed to compromise? It wouldn't be the first time.'

'It's a possibility, Edward,' Sterling answered sitting forward in her chair. 'But how does it alter anything? We're still no nearer tracking either Silver or Tamara down. All I know is what Marie told me; that Tamara was taken someplace via Amsterdam and that the Hell's Angels were somehow involved. Other than that, we've got nothing to go on.'

'And what about you, Mr Barrett?' said the cardinal taking a sip out of his brandy glass. 'You're a detective I hear. What's your take on all of this?'

Simon shifted uneasily in his seat. The events of the past couple of days had unsettled him to such a degree that he honestly didn't know what to believe.

'I was thinking,' he said before hesitating…

'Mmm, yes, go on detective,' murmured de Valois cupping his brandy glass on his lap in both hands. His gaze was as steady as a candle flame, giving Simon the distinct impression that the wily old cleric was looking straight through him rather than at him.

'I was thinking that I might make some discreet enquiries with a certain Christian evangelical organisation Tamara was a member of.'

Sterling raised her eyes in despair and slumped back in her seat.

'And what organisation might that be?' asked the cardinal with growing interest.

'The Church of Eternal Life,' ventured Simon. 'It's an American outfit with branches in the UK. Tamara had joined it shortly before she went missing.'

'And you think there might be a connection?'

'It's a possibility. The guy in charge of the organisation is someone called Clive Meredith. Tamara's father showed me a press photograph taken in England with Tamara and Clive in the same shot. There were a couple of other girls in the picture too — the same girls who were with Tamara on the night she disappeared — Rebecca Hamilton and Abigail Pearson.'

'Have you managed to make contact with these two women, Mr Barrett?'

'No, I haven't. The university authorities were reluctant to divulge any information about their students. They're a bit of a closed shop when it comes to things like that. They wouldn't tell me anything about Tamara either.'

'I see. So you think Clive Meredith is your best bet?'

'Assuming that I'm able to contact him, then yes he is.'

'You're both missing the point,' interrupted Sterling.

'Tamara was kidnapped twice. Once outside Fotheringay's nightclub and then again somewhere near Jerry Skinner's flat. I've already dealt with the two goons who were involved with the nightclub snatch.'

'So, what are you trying to say?' de Valois asked, pursing his lips.

Sterling heaved an enormous sigh. 'What I'm trying to say is that we're dealing with two separate snatches. The first was the one planned directly by Jimmy Silver. When it all went wrong, courtesy of yours truly, a second plan was brought into play.'

'And...?'

'Tamara was snatched again, outside Skinner's flat when she went out to get a bottle of milk. According to Marie, some Hell's Angels were involved in the second snatch, and Tamara ended up somewhere in Amsterdam. Somewhere *underground...*'

'So, they're holding Tamara in a cellar somewhere in Amsterdam are they, Sterling? Really, you're going to have to do a lot better than that my little bloodsucker—'

'But it was Skinner who lost her, not me!'

'And it is you who must find her,' de Valois snapped back. 'As you know, a cull is currently in force. In the circumstances, I can only give a creature such as yourself a limited amount of protection outside of which I am largely powerless to act.'

'Is that a threat, Edward?'

'You've got a week,' the cardinal replied waving her out of the room with a gesture of his hand. 'Beyond that, your fate lies solely in the hands of the Holy See, and I don't need to remind you of the consequences of that my dear.'

The meeting was over. As they walked out of the room and down the wide staircase, Simon looked at Sterling. 'What are we going to do?' he said.

'I'm not sure,' replied the vampire lost in her thoughts. That she'd been shocked by the cardinal's final words was more than apparent in the way she kept avoiding Simon's gaze. Terrified would have been a more apt description of her mental state as they descended the staircase and walked out into the cold October air.

'Underground,' she kept on muttering to herself. 'Underground...'

'What's that, Sterling?'

'Uh... oh, nothing, Simon. I was just mulling over what Marie said back there in the cemetery last night. Is Tamara being held prisoner in a cellar or a crypt?'

'Oh, right. I see.'

'Amsterdam is a big place as well.'

'I wouldn't know, Sterling. I've never been there myself.'

'Well, I have, and I'm telling you, Tamara is going to be bloody hard to find.'

'So, what's your plan then?'

'The Hell's Angel connection, that's what. Joe Rackham's gang have got contacts in the Netherlands. Maybe he knows something about it. I wouldn't put it past him if he did.'

'What about Clive Meredith?'

'What about him?'

'Maybe he's in on it too. I've dealt with this sort of thing in the States. Rich kids being kidnapped and brainwashed by religious cults. It happens all the time.'

'Yeah, well it doesn't happen in England, Simon. Us Brits don't do God, remember?'

'Oh, yes of course. I was forgetting. I'm in England now. Sorry Sterling...'

12

'Who told you that, Sterling?'

'I can't reveal my sources, Joe. All I know is that the Hell's Angels have been implicated in the kidnapping of Tamara Sheridan and I've got a week to find her.'

'And she's being held in Amsterdam, you say?'

'For the umpteenth time, Joe, yes! She was taken to Amsterdam and some Hell's Angels were involved.'

'Well, it's got nothing to do with the Harlow chapter, Sterl. My boys don't go in for that sort of thing.'

'So, who does and what do you know about the Amsterdam bikers?'

'Oh, we do some business with them, it's true, but nothing like what you're suggesting. It's mostly just a bit of crystal meth and stuff.'

'Anything else?'

'Maybe a few illegal weapons, but Spike usually handles that end of things. I'm officially retired as you know.'

The vampire sighed and stubbed out her cigarette in the ashtray. Simon could tell she was pissed off and made to offer some comment, but Skinner shook his head rapidly. 'Not now, Simon,' he said quietly. 'Not now.'

They were sitting in Skinner's flat in Islington and they were all getting nowhere fast. Sterling went silent for a while. Then:

'Phone them, Joe.'

'Who?'

'The Amsterdam mob. Phone them and give it to them straight.'

'I can't do that.'

'Why not?'

'Because it's not done, Sterling. At least, not among the Angels at any rate. We don't normally meddle in each other's business.'

'Bikers' code, huh?'

'Yeah. It's a matter of honour.'

Sterling made to laugh but all that came out of her mouth was a feral growl.

'Who's their leader?'

'I can't tell you that, Sterling.'

'Who's their fucking leader, Joe? Tell me—'

'All right. It's a guy called David Kessler. He's head honcho over there as far as the Dutch authorities are concerned. Holland is almost exclusively Hell's Angels territory and Amsterdam is the mother chapter for all the HA groups in Europe.'

'Where does he hang out?'

'He doesn't. He's a difficult bloke to pin down these days. Likes to keep a low profile, if you know what I mean. He's also got connections with the Far Right in Germany and Austria.'

'Sounds like a regular mover and shaker, Joe. How can I contact him?'

'You're joking of course.'

Sterling said nothing but looked at Joe hard.

'Okay,' he replied, 'but it won't be easy. Kessler doesn't normally give interviews. I usually call one of his gang members if I need to discuss anything with him. Other than that, he's almost impossible to locate.'

'Hmm, I see. And exactly how big are the Hell's Angels in Holland?'

'Bigger than you'd think, Sterling. When they first started up, the Dutch police just ignored them as some quirky little biker cult from America. It was only when the bodies started piling up that they began taking them seriously.'

'So, we're dealing with a sophisticated outfit then?'

'Yeah. Over the years they've become a powerful force within the Dutch underworld, so much so that politicians and businessmen used to mingle with them at various gala events and functions in the capital, though these days they tend to give them a wide berth on account of their sinister reputation.'

'How sinister?'

'Well, it's like I said. Kessler has got connections with the Far Right, and the group as a whole has dealings with the Columbian drug cartels. Politicians tend to shy away from that sort of thing.'

'What about Jimmy Silver? Do they have connections with him as well?'

'I wouldn't know, Sterling. You'll have to ask them that yourself.'

The vampire creased her brow in thought. Joe knew what was coming next and glanced at Skinner anticipating her answer.

'Get your boys together, Joe,' she said. 'We're going to Holland.'

At that, Skinner stood up from his seat and squared his shoulders at her:

'No way! You're not messing with the Angels—'

'We don't have a choice, Jerry. It's on top for the lot of us if we don't sort this thing out.'

'How do you mean?'

'Wheels within wheels, Jerry. Cardinal de Valois has powerful friends within the British establishment.'

'Since when has that ever bothered you, Sterling?' countered Joe.

'Since I found out that Edward de Valois is a member of the Order of Exorcists.'

'So…?'

'They know what I am, Joe. There's a cull in force at the moment and I can only survive it if I co-operate with the Church.'

'I see. So, de Valois has you in his pocket then?'

'In a manner of speaking, yes he has.'

'What happens if you don't play ball?' chipped in the detective, not wishing to be left out of the conversation.

'That's an easy one, Simon. I end up like that pile of shit you saw on the hallway carpet in Tamara's flat, that's what!'

'Oh… I see.'

'Yeah, what else did you expect?'

Suitably admonished, the detective looked away, prompting Joe to offer an alternative suggestion. 'Okay,' he said. 'You're obviously up to your neck in it, Sterl, so why not take up Simon's offer of checking out this Clive Meredith geezer, first? It seems to me like he's at the bottom of things somehow. If he's not, then maybe I can get a few of my chaps to help out, but I'm not promising anything mind you. If it's anything like that last caper you got us involved with down on the south coast, then I'd be surprised if you get any volunteers at all. Gordon Dyer's still having nightmares about it and

Ronnie Frinton always sleeps with the bedside light on and a gun under his pillow. You certainly rattled their bollocks for them with that little escapade of yours.'

'Thanks, Joe. You're a diamond. I'll see what I can squeeze out of Clive Meredith then I'll give you a call. I doubt if me and Simon will have much luck though, so keep your passports handy. It's likely Amsterdam may still be our best option.'

13

Just what was it about religion that made him so uptight, he wondered?

Simon had been with Sterling at the headquarters of the Church of Eternal Life for well over three hours and in spite of a considerable effort on both their parts, they'd got absolutely nowhere in their attempt to locate Clive Meredith, the organisation's charismatic leader. Later on, they'd been invited to attend an evangelical rally at a concert hall in North London where upwards of five thousand people had been in attendance, lapping up the manic rantings of all the guest preachers on stage as if it were the only thing that mattered in the whole wide world.

He was glad when they finally left the auditorium and Sterling made a call from her mobile, pacing up and down the street outside until she got a signal. 'Jerry, is that you?' she said. 'We got absolutely nowhere with the crazies. Tell Joe to bring whatever men he can muster and meet me outside the warehouse tomorrow morning at eight o'clock. We're going to Holland. It's the only way.'

***

Amsterdam was beautiful but cold. An east wind was blowing as they stood staring down into the dark waters of the Prinsengracht canal pondering what their next move should be.

'So, that's it then,' said Simon to Sterling. 'Jerry can't come.'

'Yep.'

'Nor, Joe either?'

'Nope.'

'What about those two guys Gordon and Ronnie — why aren't they available?'

'Gordon wasn't available at short notice and Ronnie's doing time in Parkhurst for grievous bodily harm. Face it, Simon, we're on our own.'

'It's a pity you didn't bring that gun of yours, Sterling. I've a feeling we might be needing it.'

'I couldn't get it through bag-check. It would have shown up on the scanner.'

'You reckon Silver's got some back-up then?'

'Yeah, by the shedload I expect, but that's not all.'

'Why, what's the problem?'

'I've a feeling we're being watched. It's been that way ever since we got off the plane at Schiphol. Someone tracked us through the airport then followed our taxi on the motorway. They were riding a motorcycle and it was no ordinary bike either.'

'Hell's Angels?'

'More than likely. He wasn't wearing his colours but that doesn't mean anything. The Angels prefer to keep a low profile these days.'

'So, what do we do now?'

'Now, Simon? Well, now we find ourselves a cheap hotel and bed down for the night. We've got a long day ahead of us tomorrow. This guy, Kessler is proving to be a bit more elusive than I thought.'

The room was quite small even by the standards of a two-star hotel, but at least it had a bathroom where Simon could take a shower and try to relax.

Relax. How could he relax when he was sharing a bedroom with that *thing* in the black leather jacket and eye shades? He'd never got used to her, and the thought of him falling asleep with an arch-predator like Sterling for company was making him feel decidedly uneasy. His fears were confirmed when he woke up at around two o'clock in the morning to find her standing beside his bed looking down on him with a hungry expression of her face.

'Shh,' she smiled placing a finger to her lips. 'Don't worry, Simon, you're not on the menu. I haven't fed in a while, that's all. I'm going out hunting tonight and I may be some time. Don't wait up for me, okay.'

And with that, she was gone. Out into the night without so much as a gesture of farewell, leaving the detective shaking and alone in his bed with a feeling that he'd just had a very narrow escape. Switching on the bedside light, he reached out for the packet of cigarettes she'd left behind and lit one up even though he'd never smoked in years. Then he switched on the radio for the BBC World Service. It wasn't an American channel, but at least it had the effect of calming him down sufficiently to stop his heart from pounding its way out of his chest. Just where was she going, he wondered? More to the point, just what exactly was it that she was going to do? It didn't bear thinking about. Maybe a shot of whisky from the minibar might help? Yes, that should do it, he thought, then maybe he could think of getting some sleep. He certainly needed it. Needed it real bad.

***

Alone. I always like to hunt alone, she thought. Simon's a nice enough guy but he would only queer my pitch and frighten off the game. I need all my wits about me in a city like this. Take them down nice and quiet. No screaming. Can't afford to make any mistakes. Nowhere to hide.

Halting at a street corner, she sniffed the air. Beyond the canal lay the Leidseplein district, one of the oldest and outermost parts of Amsterdam. Off in the distance, the electric sky signs on tall buildings glowed warmly through the October murk, while closer to hand, the lights of late-night bars and restaurants still illuminated the little spaces of the boulevards on which they stood, throwing up in silhouette the figures who sat at their respective tables sipping their drinks, eating their food and transacting the business of the night. This was where she needed to be.

Not long. Barely five minutes had elapsed before a smartly dressed businessman came up to her and asked for her name.

'It's Julie,' she replied with a false smile. 'I'm from England.'

He ordered her a drink followed by another and then they wandered off in the direction of a nearby hotel which the man had pre-booked in the anticipation of a night of pleasure.

Walking down a quiet side-street, Sterling glanced momentarily behind her then went into a lover's embrace, pressing the man up against the wall as she did so. The man was surprised. Sex workers usually didn't do this sort of thing. In an instant, she cupped one of her hands beneath his chin while clamping the other firmly behind the back of his head.

He struggled to free himself but her grip was too strong. 'Don't fight it, honey,' she whispered into his ear. 'Don't fight it...' Then she snapped his neck and sank her rapidly extending fangs deep into the side of his throat, savouring the better part of a litre of warm blood before dropping him to the ground and sauntering off down the alleyway towards the main street as if nothing had happened at all. A police car drove slowly by, its side window winding down as it drew to a halt. 'You all right, miss?' enquired the officer inside, concerned that such a young woman should be out walking the street so late at night. 'Never felt better,' she replied with a smile. 'Don't worry about me. I can handle myself.'

The policeman shrugged and wound up his window. Sterling watched as the tail lights of the vehicle receded into the distance; then she made her way on towards her next destination. It was a small shop situated near the Amstelveld market. A nondescript sort of a place dealing in herbal medicines and potions for the Chinese market. The shop was closed and shuttered up for the night, but a small sliver of light shining from within told her that someone was still up and about. Taking a coin from her pocket, she rattled it three times across the metal shutters and waited.

'Yes, who is it?' came a voice as dry as sandpaper from inside.

'It's Sterling,' she replied. 'Cardinal de Valois sent me.'

There was a pause followed by the sound of padlocks being opened and a bolt being drawn. As the shutters slowly raised, she was greeted by the sight of a diminutive oriental gentleman wearing a navy blue smock. His lined and sallow features suggested an elderly man of Cantonese extraction.

'What is it you want?' said the man, glancing nervously

up and down the street.

'A moment of your time, if I may,' answered Sterling, examining the man carefully. She was aware she was in the presence of a being who was not altogether human, but she couldn't put her finger on exactly what manner of creature he actually was. It was the ears that bothered her the most. The last time she'd seen ears like that was in a *Star Wars* movie and they'd belonged to Yoda.

'You'd better come in,' the creature replied. 'The place is in a bit of a mess, I'm afraid. I was doing some stocktaking shortly before you arrived. I don't get much time to sort things out these days.'

The interior of the shop was dark and close, its ceiling barely a foot above her head. A rich variety of herbs and spices hung from the rafters, filling the room with their exotic aroma.

'My name is Liu Xiang,' said the wizened hominid, 'but you can call me Liu. Follow me.'

The spiral staircase was shadow upon shadow until it reached the first floor landing where a swatch of lamplight spilled across the carpet from a half-open doorway. 'This is where I live,' the creature announced, pushing open the door to reveal a dimly lit chamber who's only source of illumination was a solitary electric lamp placed atop of a small octagonal table. Two armchairs, a coffee table and an old-fashioned radio were the only other items of furniture in the room. An oriental sleeping mat lay on the floor by the window.

'Permit me to offer you some refreshment, Sterling. It's not very often I have such distinguished visitors as yourself.'

Going into what passed for a kitchen, the dwarf-man busied himself for a short while, eventually returning with a heaped tray. 'Some tea and seedcake,' he beamed, placing the tray on the coffee table in front of her. 'Always refreshing at any time of the day.'

Sitting himself down in an armchair at least three times too big for him, he regarded Sterling closely.

'I take it you are a member of the undead, Miss Sterling.'

'You know?'

'Yes. I can smell a vampire from miles away and your aura is almost as dark as your soul. It's as sure a sign as any.'

Sterling grinned, showing her teeth: 'And you, Liu — what manner of creature are you?'

'Me? Oh, I'm what you Westerners call a changeling. Part goblin and part human. We live for a long time just like you vampires. Almost indefinitely in fact.'

'How long?' enquired Sterling, fascinated to be in the presence of a kindred spirit.

The changeling snorted; 'Well, let's just say that I was around when China still looked like China and leave it at that, shall we? Now, what is it that I can do for you, my dear?'

'I need a potion that will induce a miscarriage.'

Liu Xiang raised an eyebrow. 'You are in trouble, vampire?'

'It's not for me.'

'Ah, a human female. I see. Is she a friend of yours?'

'Not really. More of an acquaintance if truth be told.'

The changeling furrowed his brow. Then, brushing some crumbs of seedcake from his smock, he stood up. 'One moment,' he declared. 'I think I may have just the thing you need.'

Sterling watched as he pattered off back downstairs on his small, misshapen legs. For one so old, he moved with an athletic grace. When he returned, he was clutching a small paper bag with something concealed inside.

'Here,' he said. 'This is a special herb we use in China to procure an early termination of pregnancy. It is a strong herb, so you must be careful how you make it up. Boil some water then pour it over the herb in a pot and administer it as a tea to the patient. When using it, you must remember to avoid prolonged exposure to sunlight. Ha, ha, ha, ha!'

'Sure thing, Liu,' replied Sterling appreciating his sense of humour. Taking the bag, she placed it in the inside pocket of her biker jacket then regarded him once more.

'And I was wondering if...?'

'You were wondering if I might provide you with a gun, am I correct?'

'How did you — oh, I see.'

'Yes, Sterling. Creatures like myself have a certain degree of telepathy and prescience just like other elementals. What kind of a firearm would you be wanting?'

'Oh, just something small and easily concealed. I'm travelling across borders and don't want to get caught with one on me.'

'Going far?' enquired the changeling with a mischievous grin.

'Not sure,' replied Sterling. 'De Valois didn't mention anything about a specific location.'

'And you need to speak to someone, am I correct?' added the changeling.

'Yes. His name is David Kessler and he's the leader of a gang of Hell's Angels. Do you happen to know where I might find him?'

'No, I don't. But I might be able to point you in the right direction.'

'How do you mean?'

Liu Xiang took a sharp intake of breath and allowed his eyes to roll back in their sockets. He paused, thinking for a few moments. Then:

'The person you seek is protected by charms and spells of concealment which are not of his own making. In order to find him, you must first contact a man called Clive Meredith who is at this moment residing in the city of Amsterdam. He has an office somewhere near the cafe Mollenpad by the canal. This office functions as the headquarters of his organisation in Europe. Put enough pressure on him and he will reveal Kessler's whereabouts, of that I am certain.'

When he'd finished speaking, Liu reached into the front pocket of his smock and pulled out what looked like an old-fashioned fountain pen. Placing it on the table in front of her, he looked at Sterling with his black, piercing eyes.

'What's that for?' she exclaimed warily. 'Do you want me to sign a contract or something?'

'Good heavens, no,' the changeling replied. 'It's that gun you wanted. I knew you were going to ask me for one even before I went downstairs, so I brought you this.'

'That's a gun?'

'It's a gun-pen to be precise. You did say you wanted something small and easily concealed. Well, this is just the job.'

'How does it work?'

Liu leaned forward in his chair, his diminutive little feet barely touching the floor. 'It fires a single .22 calibre bullet and can only be used in emergencies. The firing mechanism is in the top of the pen. Turn the cap in an anticlockwise direction and pull it back until you hear a click. Now it's ready to fire.

All you need do is point it at the target and push the cap in. Bang!'

Sterling picked up the weapon and ran it through her fingers. 'What's a man like you doing with something like this, Liu? It's the sort of gun spies normally use.'

'And vampire hunters, Sterling. The bullets it fires are usually made of silver.'

Sterling stiffened in her chair but Liu motioned her to remain calm.

'Relax. De Valois told me all about it. He said I had to help you out. Had it been otherwise, you would never have left this room alive. My only concern would have been the stench of your rapidly decaying corpse and the means of its disposal. An acid bath is my preferred method of choice, though I have several others in case you were interested.'

'Thanks, Liu. You're a real diamond, you are.'

'Don't mention it, Sterling. Now, if you have nothing further to discuss might I suggest that we bring this meeting to a close. I'm not getting any younger and I need my sleep. These little legs of mine are beginning to fail me and I can sense the shadows closing in. Perhaps another century or so and I will be no more. I shall see you to the door and bid you farewell. Good luck in your quest to find David Kessler, and please remember to give Jimmy Silver my regards the next time you see him. I've been trying to kill him for years.'

14

Simon watched as the waiter brought two steaming hot cups of Americano over to where he and Sterling were seated beside the canal. It was still early morning and the café Mollenpad was bustling with commuters, all of them eager to snatch a quick coffee before attending to the business of the day. Placing both cups down on the table, the waiter smiled and departed with his tip.

'You had me worried last night, Sterling. Standing beside my bed like that, you gave me quite a fright I can tell you.'

'Sorry, Simon. Remind me to be more considerate next time.'

They both went quiet for a while as a man sat down at a table close by. He didn't stay long. Downing a small espresso, he took out his mobile phone, made a short call then continued on his way. Once he was out of earshot, Sterling carried on with the conversation:

'Liu was a hunter, Simon. I was sharing the same room with a vampire hunter and I didn't know it.'

'Growing careless in your old age, I expect.'

'Not funny. I was within an inch of my life in that room.'

'But you're okay now.'

'Yeah. Just a bit rattled, that's all. I should have known better, dammit.'

'Don't be too hard on yourself. You can't win 'em all.'

'That's all right for you to say, Simon, but you don't get

to end up as a pile of smouldering ash on someone's living room carpet, do you? He could have shot me clean through the chest with a silver bullet any time he wanted.'

'But he didn't.'

'No, but one day they'll catch up with me and then it's all over.'

She began trembling and lit up a cigarette, nervously flicking her ash into the canal below. Simon placed a reassuring hand on her shoulder to calm her down. This never happens in the movies, he thought — main protagonist comforts vampire and all is well. But it wasn't the movies, was it? He really was sitting at the table of a café in Amsterdam with his hand placed on the shoulder of a demon from hell; if that was what Sterling truly was.

Somehow, he didn't think so. Somehow, he caught a glimpse of the person, Sterling used to be — Julie Kent, the young music student from 1977. God, but that was ever such a long time ago. Before he was even born in fact. What memories lay buried behind those dark, mirrored sunglasses of hers, he wondered? Had she had dreams and ambitions once? A partner or a girlfriend perhaps? She never talked about it. Too painful more than likely… *or too long ago.*

'Clive Meredith is in Amsterdam, Simon. He's got an office somewhere near this café. Liu told me.'

'Why didn't you say?'

'You didn't ask me.'

'Uh… oh, right.'

Did she do it deliberately to annoy him, or was it just her way, Simon wondered? He couldn't begin to fathom how creatures like Sterling actually thought. Perhaps they lived so much in the present that any need for lengthy causal explanations had become a secondary concern to them. It certainly seemed that way.

'Where is he?'

'Somewhere near this café. Liu didn't give me a precise location, so we'll have to do a bit of footslogging if you feel up to it.'

'What's the time?'

'About eight thirty, give or take a few minutes. Why?'

'I need another coffee.'

'Okay, but then we go, right?'

'Yeah. Then we go.'

***

The receptionist looked up from her screen to see two strangers, a man and a woman, enter the building. Frowning, she glanced at her desk diary. It showed no appointments for that time of the day.

'Can I help you?'

The man spoke first. 'We're here to see Clive Meredith.'

'Have you made an appointment?'

'No, but he'll see us anyhow,' snapped the woman who accompanied the man. She was much younger than her partner but had a mean expression on her face. Her eyes were concealed by a pair of mirrored sunglasses that reflected all the light back into the room. She was wearing a black leather motorcycle jacket, blue jeans and biker boots.

'I'm afraid, Mr Meredith is busy at the moment and—'

'Call him anyway,' demanded Sterling abruptly

The receptionist glared at the woman then picked up her phone. In less than half a minute, a door opened and a man stepped out. He stared in surprise at the two strangers for a moment before turning to the receptionist.

'Who are these people?'

'I don't know, Mr Meredith. They haven't made an appointment, but—'

'We've got some questions we'd like to ask you, Clive,' cut in Sterling again. 'It won't take long.'

The well-groomed evangelist was uncertain how he should react to the two strangers who had just blagged their way into his inner sanctum. They looked like they belonged to an episode of NCIS rather than the usual sort of people he dealt with. The man was tidy enough in his suit and overcoat, but the woman…?

'What do you want?' he asked nervously.

Sterling nodded in the direction of the open door. 'A few moments of your time, Mr Meredith and then we shall go.'

Clive Meredith motioned to the girl at the desk that all was well and ushered the pair into his office. Once they were inside, the man in the suit and overcoat closed the door quietly behind him and stood with both feet spread on the carpet in a power position.

The woman stepped forward. There was something oddly non-human in the way she moved but he couldn't figure out what.

'My name is Sterling, Mr Meredith and my associate here is called Simon Barrett. As to what we want — we want some information which we believe you may possess.' She gestured to the filing cabinets beside the window. 'Check them out, Simon.'

Simon nodded and began sifting his way through Clive's files as if he'd done it all his life.

'You can't do that!' exclaimed the startled evangelist reaching for the phone. Sterling closed her hand around the man's wrist. 'I can do anything I like,' she replied menacingly before slowly relaxing her grip. 'Now, why don't you tell us where David Kessler hangs out? We'd like to ask him a few questions about an American woman called Tamara Sheridan.'

Clive's heart skipped a beat. Now he knew why she seemed so strange. It was the way she walked, the way she talked, seemingly impervious to his threats. A person used to having her every word obeyed. Very much like Kessler and his boss, Jimmy Silver. Now he knew what Sterling really was.

He tried to make a run for it but she was too quick for him. Sidestepping her way around his desk, she threw him against the wall, narrowly missing Simon who was still hard at work rifling through the files. When she finally grabbed him, it was with all the precision of a crocodile seizing on its prey. Then she pulled him towards her until their faces were almost touching. Smiling, she revealed her fangs, white as bone and hard as steel.

Clive made a whimpering sound in his throat. He'd never been this close to one before and he was terrified. He was also aware that his feet were now dangling clear of the floor and that he was having difficulty in breathing.

'I... I perceive that you are *not as other women,* Miss Sterling,' he said in a choked whisper.

'That is correct, Mr Meredith,' replied the vampire staring directly into his face. 'And you will tell me exactly where it is that I may find David Kessler, isn't that so?'

Clive hesitated, uncertain as to which fate might prove the worse. Instant death at the hands of this uncompromising ice-maiden, or the inevitable consequences of betraying David

Kessler and his master Jimmy Silver. Sensing his indecision, Sterling hauled him around the office and dumped him unceremoniously into his swivel chair: 'I want answers now!' she snarled, leaning over his desk and banging the palm of her hand down hard on its walnut veneer.

Clive rallied. He'd made his choice and decided he didn't want to face Kessler or Jimmy Silver.

'How dare you come into my office unannounced!' he bellowed. 'Get out now the pair of you or I'll call the police!'

Sterling smiled and seated herself down in one of the chairs reserved for his clients. 'Touch that phone and I will rip your head off, is that clear?'

The evangelist blanched and retracted his hand from the phone. 'How much do you want?'

'I don't want your money, Clive. I just want to know the whereabouts of David Kessler and Jimmy Silver, that's all.'

When there was no reply, Sterling sighed and placed both her feet on the evangelist's desk, crossing them at the ankles. 'Mr Meredith, you know what I am capable of and what I can do to your mind. I could peel it away like the layers of an onion and get all the information I want that way. You've probably seen Kessler do it to all those who have crossed him, so you know what the outcome can be.'

Clive pulled a paper tissue from a box on his desk and mopped his brow.

'They'll kill me.'

'So will I, Mr Meredith, if you don't give me the information I seek.'

'It's not fair. I was forced into procuring those women and I—'

'Those women, Clive — you mean there were others?'

The evangelist lowered his head. He knew the game was up.

'I... I didn't do anything—'

'How many, Clive?'

'Nine or ten, not many more than that.'

Simon murmured in disgust: *'Jesus fucking Christ...'*

Sterling removed her boots from the desk and leaned forward grabbing Clive by his tie. 'Do you know what they do to men like you in prison, Mr Meredith?'

The evangelist swallowed hard. 'Look, I can explain everything...'

'There's nothing to explain, Clive. You've been engaged in people trafficking, procuring women for senior vampires like Jimmy Silver, am I not correct?'

Clive nodded weakly. 'He made me do it. I had no choice.'

'But you accepted his money.'

Clive nodded again. 'Yes.'

'And you know where he lives?'

'No, I don't. I've purchased several properties on his behalf in Europe over the past few years or so, but I don't know where he is now.'

The evangelist decided he'd had enough. Even if he told her the whereabouts of Jimmy Silver, she would probably kill him anyway so what did he have to lose? Waiting for her to release her grip on his tie, he reached into the cavity shelf of his desk and felt for the handle of his revolver. It would be easy. He could say they were a couple of intruders intent on milking him for protection money. Either that or they were a pair of crack addicts trying it on for a quick fix. It would be his word against a couple of dead people. His secretary would back him up. She always did.

'Not so fast!'

It was Simon who yelled, grabbing Clive by the forearm. He'd seen what the guy was about to do and had reacted quickly. In one swift move, he prised the weapon out of the evangelist's hand and gave it to Sterling. 'Here,' he said. 'He was going to use this on you.'

Sterling examined the gun and smiled. 'Thinking of making it a head shot were you Clive? It's the only thing that would have worked on a creature like me. You knew that, didn't you?'

The evangelist looked away, reluctant to admit what he'd had in mind even though it was patently obvious that he'd meant to kill her. Turning the weapon over in her hand, Sterling regarded him coldly.

'If you don't know where Silver is then maybe you can tell me where Kessler hangs out. I know he's somewhere in Amsterdam. Perhaps you would be good enough to fill in the details for me.'

Clive shook his head vigorously. 'I can't.'

Sterling arched an eyebrow. 'Not even if I scramble your brains for you, hmm?'

'No! No way!!'

'Oh well, in that case, what if I were to break all the fingers of your right hand with the butt of this gun — would you tell me then, hmm?'

'No need, Sterling,' cut in Simon. 'I've found Kessler's address. It's in his file here.'

The vampire turned to her accomplice. She seemed disappointed.

'Tell me, Simon.'

'It's a place called The Crypt and it's situated in the

Leidseplein district.'

'A nightclub?'

'Something like that. It's likely the Hell's Angels have adopted it as their clubhouse.'

'Is that true, Clive?' she enquired, turning back to the trembling evangelist.

The man nodded slowly, now more terrified of Sterling's reaction than any future fear of what Kessler might do to him.

'You were holding out on me, weren't you, Clive?'

He nodded again.

'So, what do you think I should do with you?'

'I... I don't know.'

Sterling removed her sunglasses and gazed directly into the man's eyes. Then she slid his gun towards him across the table. Simon looked away as the evangelist sat bolt upright in his chair, paralyzed by the woman's hypnotic stare.

'Here's your gun back, Clive,' she said quietly, not once taking her eyes off him. 'When my friend and I leave this room, I want you to wait for five minutes then pick up this gun, put it in your mouth and pull the trigger. Do you understand?'

Clive nodded. Locked in his trance, he could do nothing else but obey her command.

Satisfied her request would be carried out, Sterling replaced her sunglasses and got up from her seat. 'Come on, Simon. Let's go find David Kessler. I think we're just about done here.'

With that, she turned and walked out of the office, the detective following closely in her wake.

A few moments later, Clive heard the front door of the reception area shut. He slumped back in his chair shaking with fear. He hadn't betrayed his boss, but that didn't mean Silver wouldn't find out about him betraying Kessler's whereabouts. There was nowhere he could run to and no place to hide. Sitting forward, he reached for the gun. Only a couple of minutes to go and then it would be all over. In an odd sort of way, he felt relieved.

As they walked down the street, Simon heard a muffled gunshot from the direction of Clive's office. He looked at Sterling who just shrugged. 'So, what did you find out about David Kessler?' she enquired as they continued on their way.

'Kessler was born in 1975 in Eindhoven, a small industrial city in southern Holland. He drifted through high school and developed an interest in playing billiards, hanging out in pool halls where he also dealt in drugs and mingled with the outlaw subculture of those times. Then in 1992, he went missing for a while, being placed on the police register of missing persons until his reappearance in 1997. When he resurfaced, he was a changed man. He often seemed like a guy who wasn't really there at all. Kind of distant and hard to figure out, if you know what I mean.'

Sterling smiled and let the detective continue with his narrative.

'He made his money running errands for middle-ranking drug traffickers — a dangerous occupation that frequently landed him in dicey situations. He was once stabbed in a ripped drug deal in an Amsterdam apartment but managed to make his escape by jumping out of a fourth-floor window without sustaining any apparent injury to himself.'

'That sounds like our vampire, Simon. Keep going; it's all starting to sound horribly familiar.'

'Okay. So, in 1998, Kessler was finally arrested and thrown into jail. While in prison, he met an Amsterdam club owner who'd been jailed for smuggling cannabis. The smuggler was well connected with the Hell's Angels and when Kessler was released from prison, he was invited to stay in the man's apartment for a while where he developed a link with the bikers.'

'And after that, it was only a question of time before he took them over, am I correct?'

'Yes, Sterling. How did you know?'

'It's the way all vampires work — the ones who survive the change, that is. The only question is; how did he end up in thrall to Jimmy Silver as part of his criminal network?'

'Maybe you can ask him that when we catch up with him. I suggest we visit this place called The Crypt early in the evening. That's probably the best chance we have of finding him in. Any later and the club will be rammed with customers. We can't risk a clash with all those innocent people around.'

Sterling made a low, growling sound in the back of her throat. 'No one's innocent, Simon. We all have our secrets. Come on, let's get another coffee. I saw a good marijuana café earlier on. We both need to chill out.'

***

The gang hadn't expected this.

Her hair was shoulder-length and as black as midnight. She wore a black leather jacket and a T-shirt one size too big for her. The legs of her faded blue jeans were tucked into a pair of low-heeled biker boots. And, of course, there were the mirrored sunglasses that always concealed her eyes.

She stood blocking the doorway of the club with her head tilted to one side. Her heart was pounding in her chest and her body was trembling with adrenalin. She'd made the mistake of sending Simon in first and now she had to rectify the situation. What was more, there was no sign of David Kessler anywhere in the room. All the people in the club had human auras, albeit a good deal diminished by a lifetime of hard drugs and alcohol. Of the dark crimson aura of a vampire there was no sign.

'What are you going to do about it bitch?' said the fat Dutchman with the Hells Angels insignia on the back of his denim jacket. He had Simon cornered near a pool table with a Zombie knife and plenty of his mates to back him up.

The club was located in the basement of one of the older-style buildings facing the street. The main room had a low ceiling. It stank of stale beer and cigarette smoke. The actual bar was small and situated against the far wall beneath the only decent lighting in the joint. Several clubhouse members sat on high stools at the bar drinking lager and laughing among themselves. The rest were gathered around the pool table threatening Simon. Things were beginning to turn ugly.

'Leave him alone,' she repeated firmly as she walked downstairs into the club. She had expected to find the place inhabited solely by members of the Hell's Angels gang who ran the joint, but there were others too. The tables and benches scattered throughout the room boasted several hookers, a drug-dealer, two hard-core alcoholics and five teenage boys who were obviously prospective members of the gang. They would be the ones she had to deal with first.

A slim hand grabbed her by the elbow. 'Hey, babe. You looking for someone?'

The lad couldn't have been much more than seventeen, with straggly brown hair and acne-pitted cheeks. He wore a black T-shirt beneath his denim jacket.

Sterling shook her head. 'Just my friend over there by the pool table.'

The teenager smiled, still holding her by the elbow. The men at the bar were watching them both now, as were the others gathered around the pool table. 'You can forget that asshole, baby. I'm here now.'

She shook her head for a second time.

'No, I'm with the American over there,' she replied, slipping his grip and walking forward once again.

Sniggering laughter ran through the men at the bar. The youth blushed red and grabbed her arm more firmly than before. 'Maybe you didn't hear me right the first time,' he replied. 'I'm your friend now.'

Sterling felt her patience start to melt. It would be tempting to just give in and indulge her taste for fresh blood. Better to leave now before things got any worse and she lost control, but her friend Simon was in too much trouble and she was beginning to get thirsty again. Something had to give. It was only a matter of time.

'I don't think you're her type, Steve,' jeered one of the older men at the bar. More laughter followed. Steve's face grew redder.

'We really must be leaving now,' she said, disengaging herself for a second time.

'What's the matter, bitch? Aren't I good enough for you?'

Steve's eyes were no longer sane. For a brief moment, she scanned the boy's thoughts. Steve was the gang's pet psychotic. He may have looked like a gauche, wide-eyed teenager, but beneath that pale, acne-pitted face lurked something far more dangerous.

Fuck this, she thought. *Let's settle the fucker's hash right now.*

Still in control of the situation, she punched the boy square in the teeth and sent him sprawling to the floor with a split lip. It was then that the rest of the gang rounded on her, blocking her exit from the club.

One of the older gang members walked towards her: 'I bet you have trouble seeing with those dark glasses of yours,' he said, reaching out to snatch her shades.

Sterling's hand flashed upwards, her fingers closing around his wrist. There was a sound like splintering wood and the man began screaming. Then he sank to the floor, his face white with shock.

'Your name is Peter, isn't it?' she said, turning to look directly at the fat biker who had Simon pressed up against the wall near the pool table.

'How did you know that?' replied the biker holding the Zombie-knife at Simon's throat.

'Simple. I read your mind. Now, why don't you let my friend go before I ram that knife of yours right up your fat arse!'

The room became silent, but it wasn't because of what Sterling had just said. All eyes were now turned in the direction of the staircase. The sound of descending footsteps made it clear that someone else had just entered the club and it wasn't anyone ordinary either.

As the man reached the bottom of the stairs, everyone in the clubhouse shrank back into the shadows to let him pass. Clearly, this was a man of power; one who was used to having his every word and gesture obeyed. Walking into the centre of the room, the man looked around for a few moments until his gaze settled on Sterling, He was wearing mirrored sunglasses much like her own and his aura was crimson, indicating that he wasn't human.

'David Kessler?'

'I have that name among many others,' the man replied coolly. 'You must be the one who calls herself, Sterling, am I correct?'

She nodded slowly. A meeting between two vampires of equal power usually didn't end well. With a sweep of his hand, Kessler ordered the man called Peter to release Simon and put away his knife. The man called Peter did so without as much as a word and returned to his seat beside the bar. As the small talk in the room gradually resumed, Kessler indicated a private booth where Sterling and Simon could sit together. Then he walked over and sat himself down at the table facing Sterling with barely an arm's length between them. Instinctively, she kept one hand on the switchblade concealed inside her jacket pocket. Kessler smiled knowingly, revealing ivory teeth between thin lips. 'Your reputation precedes you, Sterling. You may put away your weapon. We are on neutral ground here.'

Simon nodded his reassurance. Up until this point, he'd been under the impression that the clubhouse was a dangerous place. Maybe his friend was only taking precautions.

'How did you know I was coming?' asked Sterling, relaxing her grip on the switchblade.

'Clive rang me shortly before he put a bullet through his brain. That was a neat trick of yours if you don't mind me saying so.'

'He had it coming.'

She could feel the energy surging through Kessler's aura. God, but he was powerful, she thought. His nimbus swirled and eddied around him, reaching out with crimson tendrils until it almost touched her own. In an equal fight, she would probably lose.

'Who's your friend?' enquired Kessler curiously.

'His name is, Simon Barrett,' she replied. 'He's an American.'

Kessler shifted his attention momentarily in Simon's direction. As he did so, the detective felt the hair on the back of his neck start to rise. A ripple of fear ran up his spine like a cobra. The Dutch vampire was probing him already.

'How much does he know?' continued Kessler, returning his gaze to Sterling.

'Enough.'

'Good. Then he will have some inkling of what we are about to discuss.'

'Depends on how far you want to go and what you have to say, Kessler.'

Just then, a waitress arrived with a bottle of Jack Daniel's and three small whisky glasses. Placing them on the table, she retreated back to the bar without collecting her tip, only too pleased to be out of the way. With a smile of satisfaction, Kessler unscrewed the metal cap of the bottle and poured out a full measure of whisky into each of the glasses, offering two of them to Sterling and Simon. 'Welcome to hell, Mr Barrett,' he exclaimed clinking his glass against Simon's. 'I hope your stay will be a pleasant one.'

'What do you mean?' enquired the detective, concerned at Kessler's use of words.

'What I mean is, welcome to the *real world,* Simon — the world which your friend, Sterling and myself inhabit. I trust she has filled you in on all the details?'

'I'm still not following you.'

Kessler glanced at Sterling. 'Why not,' she sighed returning his glance. 'He's got to learn sooner or later.'

'Okay,' continued Kessler. 'Here's the score, Simon. The world which Sterling and myself inhabit is the real world, but over the centuries you humans have somehow conditioned yourselves not to see it.'

'What — you mean the world of vampires?'

'Yes; and a whole lot more. It's the reason why humans are instinctively afraid of the dark. They know we exist but are too scared to admit it.'

'What are you saying?'

'That you are all in denial, Simon. Giving up on it because you're afraid of what you might see. It's understandable, of course. After all, you are our main prey animal. But consider all the benefits if you were permitted to walk freely in our world and see all the things that we can see. Some human psychics can do as much and so could you with a bit of training.'

'Keep your hands off him, Kessler,' growled Sterling. 'This human is under my protection. He doesn't want to end up like us.'

'Your friend still has a sense of honour, Mr Barrett,' continued the Dutchman wryly. 'One of the few human weaknesses she's got left I shouldn't wonder.'

'That's enough!' cut in Sterling once again. 'You know why I'm here and the information I require. I take it Clive briefed you before he shot himself?'

'He did.'

'And?'

'He told me that you wish to locate the whereabouts of Jimmy Silver, am I correct?'

'You are, but it's more like Tamara Sheridan I want to trace. I understand you may have had some involvement in her kidnapping and transportation.'

Kessler went silent. His aura contracted, settling around his physical body like a protective cocoon. Then he signalled for one of his minions to come over. As the man approached, Sterling tensed and waited for the clash.

'Thank you, Paul,' said Kessler accepting the small package the man obediently placed on the table in front of him. As the man departed, Simon took a good look at the Amsterdam biker. There was something strangely reptilian about the Dutchman that the detective didn't like. Something decidedly unclean and untrustworthy in the way he kept glancing nervously around the room. Maybe it was just his way, but somehow Simon knew that if it came to a fight, he would side with Sterling whatever the outcome. This man, David Kessler had no sense of honour at all — even for a member of the undead.

'What's in the package, Kessler?' hissed his vampire friend. It was more of a snarl really and maybe her way of signalling that she was pissed off.

'It's a present for you, Sterling. A token of my appreciation... and respect.'

'What for?'

'For getting rid of Jimmy Silver for me. What else?'

Kessler was smiling now. He had the English vampire exactly where he wanted her and wasn't about to let her off the hook. She was about to unwrap the package when Simon grabbed her by the arm.

'No! It's a trap. Don't accept it.'

Sterling shrugged him away and removed the wrapping

from the parcel. Then she opened the cardboard box inside. Pulling out what looked like a small plastic hand-tool, she examined it carefully.

'What's this?' she said, playing the orange object through her hands.

'It's a cordless nail gun,' replied, Kessler. 'You'll need it when you get to Germany.'

'I'm going to Germany?'

'Yeah, that's where Jimmy Silver lives now. You did want to know the whereabouts of Tamara Sheridan, didn't you?'

'Yes, but—'

'Well then, you'll have to kill Silver in order to rescue her, won't you? Unless of course, she's already dead... or should I say, *undead.*'

'Not funny, Kessler. Why do you want, Jimmy dead?'

'For the same reason as you do, Sterling. Revenge. Neither of us chose to be the way we are. Your hatred of Jimmy Silver is legendary among our kind and now I'm offering you a chance to kill him, that's all.'

'There's more to it than that, David. What's the real reason you want Jimmy out of the picture?'

The Dutch revenant slammed his whisky glass down on the table. 'Power, that's what! Jimmy once told me the only thing worth having in this world of ours is power and he was right. In this century, money is power and the quickest way to get it is through the proceeds of organised crime, which is why I run this little operation of mine here in Amsterdam as head of the local branch of the Hell's Angels. The Angels got busted globally by the feds back in 2003 so nobody thinks we're a threat any more. It's the perfect cover really.'

'But it's not the full story, is it?' put in Simon quietly. He'd been listening intently to Kessler's speech and wasn't entirely convinced that control of the regional narcotics trade was all the Dutchman had in mind.

'Yes. What's in it for me, Kessler?' added Sterling taking a gulp of whisky from the Dutchman's glass.

'Simple,' he replied. 'You get to run the British end of the market along with Joe Rackham and we split the profits three ways.'

'And the nail gun? Where does that come in?'

'It's no ordinary nail gun, Sterling. The nails it fires are silver plated; just the thing for dealing with Jimmy, or any other vampire for that matter. It's also easier to smuggle across borders than a real gun. Fill old Jimmy full of 3mm silver tacks and he's bound to croak sooner or later. His assassination will have taken place during a general cull, so others of our kind will automatically assume that it was the Vatican who ordered the hit. None of them will be any the wiser and the two of us will both be at liberty to seize power in the political vacuum created by his death. We shall quite literally, *rule the roost* in Europe, if you'll pardon the pun.'

'That easy, huh?'

Kessler nodded, smiling at her all the while. 'Oh, I'm not saying it would be easy, Sterling. Knowing, Jimmy as we do, I dare say he'll be well enough protected up there in his cold mountain lair.'

'You know where he is then?'

Kessler nodded again. 'Yes, he's been living in Germany if you must know. Where better for someone who bankrolls the Far Right to hang out? I can tell you his precise location if you agree to my terms.'

Quickly, Sterling fell into a whispered conversation with

Simon as Kessler looked on.

'What's your take on all of this, Simon? You reckon he's on the level?'

'How the hell should I know? I'm not familiar with vampire politics. In fact, I didn't even know you vampires had a power structure until I met that deadly little fucker over there. We could be walking straight into a trap.'

'We've got a silver nail gun...'

'Yes, and I've got one too; back in the States; except I keep mine on the tool board in my garage where it's nice and safe.'

'Cut the crap, detective. Are you in or out?'

Simon heaved a sigh. 'Okay, we've managed to get this far and I need to find Tamara just as much as you do, so I guess I'm in.'

'Drink on it?' said Sterling pouring out a liberal measure of Jack Daniel's into each of the three glasses on the table. Reluctantly, Simon raised his glass and clinked it against the others, downing the amber liquid in one go.

'That's the spirit!' exclaimed the Dutchman, patting Simon on the back. 'You're one of us now.'

The detective feigned a smile, but it wasn't fooling anyone. He was shit scared and he knew it. Sensing his fear, Sterling cut to the chase.

'Okay, Kessler; so whereabouts in Germany does Silver hang out?'

The Dutch vampire put down his whisky glass and spoke across the table in hushed tones. 'Last I heard, he was living in an old castle situated deep within the Brocken forest. The Brocken is a place in Saxony regarded as sacred by all the witches of Europe. It is a land of towering cliffs and forested valleys that are almost impossible to penetrate unless you know the area well.'

'Have you ever been to the castle?'

'Only once. Silver doesn't exactly encourage visitors and the place is strictly off-limits to tourists. Locals tend to shun the district and the area around the castle is reputed to be the haunt of werewolves. I attended a meeting there about six months ago with several Romanian mobsters. Strictly business you understand.'

'See any werewolves?' interrupted the detective half in jest.

Sterling shot him a glance. 'Werewolves are no joke, Simon. If we get caught out in the open by a pack of those things then it's curtains for the pair of us.'

'Uh, sorry Sterling. I wasn't thinking, that's all. I mean, *werewolves* — for fuck's sake!'

'Well, you didn't believe vampires were real until you met me and Kessler, did you?'

'No, but I mean—'

'Your friend is right, detective,' added the Dutchman. 'You need to watch your back if you're out in the Brocken after dark. Those bastards can tear a human being apart in a matter of seconds, I'm telling you.'

Kessler moved his hand slowly under the table, staring all the while at Sterling as he did so. He was wearing the same type of sunglasses as she was and his thin, pale face and jet-black hair almost made him a mirror image of her were it not for the small goatee beard he displayed beneath his chin.

'So, how do we get there?' she enquired, watching Kessler's right arm for any sign of movement. Something about the situation caused Simon to tense.

'Easiest way is to take the train to the town of

Wernigerode,' replied the Dutchman.

'What then?' murmured, Sterling only half-listening.

'Then you change trains at Wernigerode for the village of Schierke which lies within the Brocken forest.'

'Uh, huh. And then what do we do?' she continued, still watching Kessler's arm.

'Leaving the village of Schierke, you follow the tourist trail through the woods for about two hours until you come to some crossroads. At the crossroads, you turn right and keep on walking until you come to a privately maintained road. The castle isn't very far after that.'

'And what is this castle called? The castle must have a name, surely?'

Kessler faltered. He hadn't anticipated the question and was at a loss for words.

'What's the castle called, Kessler?' continued Sterling repeating the question firmly.

'It... it doesn't have a name. At least, not one I can recall.'

Simon gazed on. The Dutchman was blustering now. Either the castle truly didn't have a name or he was lying and had never actually been there.

'Shake on it, Kessler,' said Sterling extending her hand towards him. Hesitantly, Kessler obeyed and extended his left hand, all the while keeping his right concealed beneath the table. In one swift move, she grabbed him by the wrist and slammed his forearm down onto the boards firing the nail gun into the pale white flesh of his palm. There was a snarl of pain followed by a single gunshot, telling Simon that the Dutchman had been hiding a concealed weapon. Well, it wouldn't do him any good now, would it? Not with his left hand pinned to the table like that.

Things began to move fast. Figures came out of the shadows brandishing weapons or whatever else they could lay their hands on. One of the youths — the one called, Steve — lurched forward, wrapping his arms around Sterling's waist in an effort to grapple with her. Big mistake. She began laughing, then her knee pistoned up, smashing into his groin. He let out a piercing wail before collapsing, unaware that she'd also fractured his pelvis as well as rupturing his balls.

Another youth lunged at her, only to be grabbed by the throat and hurled against the wall with considerable force, instantly breaking his spine in two places. Now she was in her element, strutting around the centre of the room waiting for the next contender to challenge her for control of the floor.

Someone swung a baseball bat at her. It was no big deal. She just caught the bat and brought it down on her attacker's head, splitting the man's skull as she did so. Her laughter grew louder. She hadn't had this much fun in years.

The next to grapple with her was the burly, thickset leader of the pack — the one who called himself, Peter. Agile in spite of his bulk, he circled around her until he felt he had the advantage. Sterling caught a glimpse of his knife just before he plunged it between her ribs, only to have her pull it out a split second later and turn it against him with equal force, sending its blade exactly where she said she would.

'She's rammed it straight up his arse!' shouted one of the men. 'She's gone and rammed it straight up his fucking arse! I'm getting out of here.'

A police siren wailed in the distance as the man made for the exit door. Most of the others followed with the exception of one of the remaining youths who was frozen to the spot with fear. Simon knew what was coming next and looked away.

'Come here young man,' she said darkly. 'I won't hurt you.'

'I... I...' The youth was terrified beyond words as he stood there trembling near the bar like a cornered rabbit. Slowly, she walked towards him, gently soothing the barriers of his mind before he surrendered to her embrace and they huddled together like a pair of lovers on a cold winter's night.

The police sirens were getting closer now. She would have to work fast. Her fangs extended, white and hard as she pulled the boy closer. 'Will I become a vampire too?' he whimpered, catching the reflection of his terrified face in her mirrored sunglasses.

'I don't think so,' she whispered in his ear before sinking her teeth deep into the side of his neck and savouring the warm blood as it came gushing out. The boy shuddered for a few seconds and then died where he stood. She'd been kind to him. Kinder than she'd been to Kessler who now lay slumped across the table in the booth where they'd been sitting only a few seconds before. As to whether or not the toxic effects of the silver nail embedded in his hand would actually kill him, it was impossible to say. Both she and the detective would have to leave the club and make their escape as best they could before the police arrived and cordoned off the area. There was simply no other way out.

Sterling and Simon watched from an alleyway about fifty metres up the road as the police cars pulled up outside the clubhouse. The bartender, who'd been hiding behind the counter when things had turned ugly, must have phoned the police from his mobile when he heard the screaming start. Sterling and Simon had left through the rear fire exit before any of the cops had summoned up enough courage to enter the building.

'I like it when you get angry,' observed Simon as they walked away from the flashing lights and ambulance sirens.

'So do I,' replied, Sterling, rubbing the ache in her ribs where the knife had penetrated. 'Come on. Let's get out of here before they put the police tape up. We need to get to Germany fast.'

15

She found him drinking an espresso in the café across the street from their hotel. It was late afternoon and the sun was already beginning to sink behind the mountains which surrounded the town of Wernigerode on all sides. Glancing up from his table, he gestured her to take a seat. He couldn't see her eyes behind those mirrored sunglasses of hers and wondered if she was looking at him or not.

'Simon…'

'Yes?'

'Simon. It's about last night. I'm sorry.'

The detective took a sip of coffee and looked away. He felt unclean. It wasn't that he'd never played the game before, but it was usually from the other side of the tracks. She'd been rough with him in the small hotel bed where they'd spent the night, and what was more, her fangs had extended during sex causing him to panic, grab what clothes he could and run off screaming into the night.

'Where have you been?' she enquired, interested to know how he'd spent the day.

'I bought a guidebook,' he replied, returning her gaze.

'Oh…'

'It's more of a pamphlet really. Here, take a look.'

Sterling picked up the book and read the title out loud.

'*A Visitor's Guide to the Brocken*?'

'Yeah, and guess what I found on page twelve.'

'What?'

'It's a map showing the location of a castle deep within the Brocken forest. The map isn't very precise, more of a tourist guide than anything else, but there's a symbol for an ancient monument clearly shown to the west of the village of Schierke.'

'How far?'

'About five kilometres or so. And look, there's the crossroads just like Kessler said.'

As Sterling pondered the map, Simon looked around. The tourist season was a distant memory now and there weren't many people in the quaint, old-fashioned café with its cute little gothic chairs and oak-panelled walls. The whole town was like that — just like something out of an old German fairy tale, complete with Tolkien's Middle-Earth thrown in for good measure. He was almost expecting Hansel and Gretel to come walking in through the door when something caught his eye. It was a red Ferrari parked in the town square outside.

'Nice car,' he said, admiring the sleek lines of the vehicle framed in the window of the café.

'Uh?' said Sterling, only half-listening.

'That sports car out there in the square. It must have cost a fortune.'

'Oh, yeah,' she replied returning to the map. 'Some people must have money to burn.'

With his detective's intuition in overdrive, Simon gestured for a waitress to come over to their table.

'Yes, can I help you?' said the young woman producing her notepad and pen. Her English was impeccable.

'Oh, I don't want to order anything,' answered Simon with a smile. 'I was just wondering who owns that car out there in the square, that's all.'

A picture of Aryan perfection, the blonde waitress followed Simon's pointing finger. She stared as a middle-aged man crossed the square, and made his way toward the car. He was wearing a designer suit way too thin for the season, and his hair was greying at the temples. A pair of lightly tinted sunglasses concealed his eyes.

'He's an Englishman who visits the town from time to time,' replied the girl. 'He was in here about half an hour ago. Said he'd been visiting some friends in the Brocken and that he was travelling down to Italy for the winter. Calabria, I think he said.'

Something in Sterling's manner suddenly changed. She was trembling and her breath had become irregular and ragged. Simon stared at her.

'You okay?'

'It's him.'

'Who?'

'The owner of the red Ferrari. It's Jimmy Silver.'

Simon was surprised at the venom behind her voice. Even more noticeable was the attitude of the waitress who was by now regarding Sterling with a look of concern.

'Are you all right, madam?' she said. 'You look like you've just seen a ghost or something.'

Silver got into his sports car and drove off. If he noticed, Sterling seated there in the window of the café, he didn't show it. The moment the Ferrari disappeared into traffic, the emotion gripping her lessened and she was able to relax a little.

'Do you want me to call an ambulance?' said the waitress glancing at Simon. 'I think your friend here is having a panic attack.'

Sterling shook her head vigorously. 'No, I'm fine, really I am. How long does it take to get to the village of Schierke?'

'Not long. There's a train leaving in about ten minutes, you could catch it if you run.'

'And the Brocken Forest — how far is it from Schierke?'

The waitress blinked. 'You don't want to venture into the Brocken at this time of the day. It'll be dark in about four hours time and the old forest isn't a good place to be after dark. A group of backpackers went missing out there a few months ago and they still haven't been found yet.'

'Not my problem. Come on, Simon, let's go. We've got a train to catch.'

***

'Am I in a Harry Potter story or what?' exclaimed the detective as they boarded the train. It was an ancient German steam train, all black and shiny with a bright red buffer plate at the front.

'It's for the tourists,' said Sterling. 'Kind of cute, isn't it?'

'If you say so,' replied Simon seating himself down in the passenger carriage. 'How long did the booking clerk say it would take to reach Schierke?'

'About fifteen minutes or thereabouts.'

'And you're adamant we should visit this castle even though the waitress said Jimmy Silver was heading south for the winter?'

'I don't see why not. He didn't have anyone with him in the car, so maybe Tamara is being held captive in the castle by one of his minions.'

'Or maybe she's dead.'

'I seriously doubt it, Simon. Cardinal de Valois said Silver was using her to breed from.'

'So, you think he's done the dirty deed and then gone off to Italy while she incubates his vampire super-brat for him?'

'It wouldn't surprise me. It's the way most senior vampires work. They very much resemble their aristocratic forebears in that respect. At one time, half the nobility of Europe was reckoned to be contaminated with their bastards.'

'But, what about you, Sterling? Where do you fit in with all of this?'

'You mean, how was I *born?*'

'Yes.'

'I was a mistake, Simon. Jimmy Silver wasn't counting on having a granddaughter like me. You see, there are two ways a vampire can breed. The traditional way like humans do, and then the method you see portrayed in the movies; though the latter offspring usually don't survive much beyond three months. Unfortunately for Silver, I did.'

'Which would make you a strong candidate for his throne, am I not correct?'

'You've hit the nail right on the head there, Simon; which is why he's been trying to have me taken out for years, but so far hasn't met with very much success. Now I'm coming after him. I don't have very much choice in the circumstances — it's either him or me'

As the train pulled away from the platform, Sterling took the guidebook out of her shoulder bag and began reading from its pages:

'The Brocken forest is situated in the Harz mountain region of Saxony-Anhalt and contains northern Germany's highest peak known as the Brockenberg; believed to be the

sacred meeting place of all of Europe's witches on Walpurgis Night. In medieval times, the district was shunned by the local peasants and lacked any direct supervision by the aristocracy until in 1501 the Emperor Maximilian granted lordship of the region to a knight adventurer called Martin Karlsh for his services in helping to rid the area of werewolves. Karlsh was thought to have built a castle somewhere in the vicinity of the Brockenberg, deep in the heart of the forest. The castle remained in the hands of the Karlsh family until the Protestant Reformation when it was stormed by an army of local peasants and all the inhabitants slain. Thereafter, it remained a ruin until the late eighteenth century when it was occupied and restored by a certain Leopold Kammler of Hesse who was rumoured to be...'

'Yes, Sterling, I'm waiting. What was Leopold Kammler rumoured to be? A witch perhaps; or a werewolf maybe?'

'Neither, Simon.'

'Then, what?'

'Leopold Kammler was rumoured to be a vampire. And what is more, there isn't any record of the occupation of the castle after that date. Its history ends in 1789, the year of the French Revolution when Kammler disappears from the historical record.'

'So, the guy died and the place got forgotten about. It still doesn't make Kammler a vampire, does it? I remember back when I was a kid, there was this old house at the end of our street which remained unoccupied for so long it had a tree growing through the roof of its front porch. It stayed that way for years until one day it—'

'—Mysteriously caught fire and burned to the ground?'

'How did you know that, Sterling? Are you mind-reading

me again?'

'No, Simon, I'm not, but there's usually a very good reason why certain houses appear to remain unoccupied for long periods of time.'

'What are you saying?'

'I'm saying, it's more than likely that that old house at the end of your street was a vampire's lair. The fire you witnessed as a child may well have been the work of a vampire hunter who decided to torch the place after killing its inhabitant. It's usually the only way to make sure the beast is dead.'

'Uh...? Oh, I see. Come to think of it, I kind of remember there having been some mysterious murders and disappearances in the neighbourhood when I was a kid. The cops thought they might have a serial killer on their hands but they never caught anyone. The murders stopped soon after the fire I seem to recall.'

'They would.'

'So, why do you think the year 1789 was significant in the case of Leopold Kammler?'

'Because, up until that point, Kammler had enjoyed a relatively trouble-free reign in his career as a vampire. As an aristocrat, his position in society rendered him virtually immune from prosecution. He was to all intents and purposes above the law; the perfect environment for an alpha predator like himself to operate in. That all changed, however, with the outbreak of the French Revolution, when aristocrats like Kammler were forced back into the shadows along with many others like him — including our old friend, Jimmy Silver.'

'Who now owns Kammler's castle where he's holding Tamara Sheridan against her will?'

'I presume so, Simon. Humans have short memories. No

one believes in us any more. What better cover can a vampire have than disbelief — and what better time to enter his lair than while the master of the house is away on vacation.'

'But, what about the castle? We still don't know its exact location or what it's called.'

'That's where you're wrong, detective. It says in this guidebook here that the castle was originally hewn out of solid granite from one of the strange rock formations that occur in the area. So strange was it in shape that the locals called it the Hag Rock on account of it resembling an aged crone. In later times, it attracted other names, including the epithet *Labyrinthschloss,* because of its maze of gloomy passageways and seemingly endless corridors. There's even a legend attached to the castle which tells of how one day a lone woodcutter happened to stumble across the entrance to one of these passageways and vanished from the face of the earth never to be seen again until a century later, when he was found wandering in the woods stark raving mad but just as young as the day he disappeared.'

'That's impossible.'

'Well, that's what the story says.'

'Sounds like a typical German folk tale to me.'

'I wouldn't take folk tales so lightly, Simon. Remember, I'm not supposed to exist, but I do, along with a whole load of other stuff humanity prefers to brush under the carpet.'

'Yeah, but—'

'There's no *buts* about it. If you ask me, the person who built the castle knew what they were doing and probably got a local witch to put an enchantment on the place. The whole area is reputed to have been sacred to witches at one time, remember?'

'And werewolves,' grinned the detective, 'don't forget the werewolves.'

'Ah, yes — werewolves. You think they don't exist either, do you Simon?'

'I... I didn't say they didn't, I just...'

'Just what?'

'Oh, never mind. Here's our stop coming up now. The village of Schierke. It's twinned with Hell, apparently.'

***

'So, that's the castle. The guy who built it must have been off his nut!'

Simon was perched atop of a rocky precipice, squinting through some binoculars at the demonic manor house in the valley below. Not that he needed them to see Leopold Kammler's architectural nightmare — the rambling mansion practically filled the small valley beyond the crossroads until it simply petered out and merged with its forested margins on all four sides.

Sterling pointed to the centre of the brooding assemblage of gothic turrets, embattled walls and flying buttresses. 'You can still make out the original rock formation in the middle of it all. See anyone about?'

Simon shook his head and lowered his binoculars. 'No, the place looks deserted. All the shutters are closed and the courtyard is overgrown with weeds. No one's been here in years.'

'I'm not so sure. Tamara's in there somewhere. I can sense her presence.'

'What about, Silver? You reckon he doubled back on us?

He could easily have done it in that fast car of his.'

'No, Simon. Jimmy Silver isn't in there, but something else is.'

'What do you mean?' said the detective rubbing the bridge of his nose. 'I can't imagine anyone choosing to live in that crumbling mausoleum.'

Sterling made no reply. Glancing up, she looked at the evening sky. It had taken them the better part of three hours from the village of Schierke, following the narrow roads and tourist trails of the Brocken forest before they had reached the isolated valley that separated the ancient castle from the rest of the world. Now they were here, she seriously doubted her ability to confront whatever it was that was lurking down there in the rapidly darkening woods or within the gloomy confines of the castle. Anything could be in that derelict old building. She'd dealt with similar sites before in her time as a vampire and knew what manner of creatures inhabited abandoned castles. The older they were, the nastier they got. It came with the package. She was loathe to mention it to Simon, but right now her body was in serious need of some fresh blood and she wasn't too bothered where she got it from.

'Okay, let's do this,' she said at last, adjusting the straps of her shoulder bag. Simon nodded and handed Sterling the binoculars. Getting up, he brushed himself down and began the steep descent to the valley below. Soon they were standing at the crossroads looking down a long avenue of trees, stark and black against the October sky.

'That's it there,' exclaimed Simon pointing out the shape of a tall, steepled tower rising above the skyline somewhere off in the distance.

'Uh, huh,' replied Sterling. She was only half listening.

Cautiously, she paused and sniffed the air. Something else had caught her attention.

'The castle,' Simon continued, 'is dead ahead beyond that bend in the—'

The creature was on top of him, knocking him to the ground before he had a chance to finish his sentence. Whatever it was, it smelled of dog and was very mean, and very, very pissed off.

'Get it off me! Get it off me!' he shrieked, jamming his well-padded forearm into the beast's mouth to prevent its massive jaws from closing around his throat. Then he heard a growling sound, equally as feral as that made by the thing that was trying to kill him, but coming instead from Sterling as she grabbed the creature by its thick, grey fur and gamely yanked it away from him, hurling it some distance away into the bushes by the side of the road. In less than a second, the thing sprang back at her and they both fell sprawling on the ground, churning up the leaf litter in their wake. To Simon's mind, the fight resembled a desperate battle he'd once witnessed between two mauling dogs in the neighbourhood where he'd grown up. Well, it would have been like that, were it not for the fact that this creature which his friend was so bravely grappling with was no ordinary mutt. More like a wolf than any dog; with its matted grey fur and lambent eyes, the beast growled out its fury with a malice bordering on the psychotic. Then it stood up like a man, grasping Sterling around her body with both its hands, causing her legs to kick out in mid-air, in an effort to regain contact with the ground.

'The nail gun, Simon!! Get the nail gun out of my bag and shoot the damn thing! It's a fucking werewolf!'

Without stopping to think, the detective scrambled to his

feet and quickly retrieved Sterling's discarded satchel, frantically searching for the orange nail gun inside. Pulling it out, he pointed it in the direction of the fight just in time to see the giant man-wolf making ready to clamp its jaws around his friend's skull.

—Thock… Thock… Thock… Thock…!

He fired four nails in rapid succession directly into the beast's torso. Then, when it turned its huge, ugly head in his direction, he fired again. The creature howled with rage and dropped Sterling to the ground, roaring out its challenge as it rounded on Simon who was standing by the side of the road. Then, just as it was about to spring, it started trembling violently on its hind legs before slowly collapsing to the ground beneath its heavy weight. The silver nails were beginning to have their effect.

Another few seconds and the faux wolf was lying in the middle of the road having something resembling a *grand mal* seizure. 'Shoot him again!!' yelled Sterling getting up from where the beast had dropped her.

Without hesitating, the detective fired five more rounds into the creature's body, causing the werewolf to writhe and arch its back in one final massive convulsion before it finally expired.

'Is it dead?' he enquired as they both walked hesitantly towards the corpse.

'I think so. You put enough silver into that thing to keep the Federal Reserve afloat for the rest of the century. Now, come on; let's get out of here before any more of the bastards show up. It's almost night-time and that's when they come out.'

Together, they walked off down the road until they came

to a high wall. There was a massive wooden door set into the wall which they guessed must be the entrance to the castle. Behind them they could hear a rustling sound in the undergrowth which Simon put down to the breeze but which Sterling reckoned must be the werewolf pack tracking them through the forest.

'Keep that nail gun handy, Simon while I check out this door. I think we're being followed.'

'I... I haven't got it, Sterling.'

'What?'

'The nail gun; I must have dropped it back there on the trail. I'll go back and get it.'

'No, don't do that. You won't last five minutes out there on your own. Here, give me a hand getting this door open. I think it's stuck.'

Putting their shoulders to the weathered timber door, they leaned into it and pushed with all their might. Eventually, it gave way and slowly opened to reveal the overgrown courtyard Simon had glimpsed from the top of the cliff. Beyond the courtyard there was another wall, much higher and set with a series of tiny gothic windows in the German style which began at second storey height and continued upward until they reached the eaves of a precipitous roof.

'Just looking at that place is making my brain hurt,' remarked Simon as they stood examining the castle.

'That's not surprising,' observed Sterling dryly. 'The entire house is saturated with dark magic.'

'Come again?'

'Someone's put one goddam almighty spell on that castle if I'm not very much mistaken. It's not surprising Silver was using it as his lair. The whole building is functioning under some kind of protective charm to ward off intruders — and not your normal sort of intruders either. No wonder the Vatican couldn't locate him. He was operating entirely off their radar. As far as they were concerned, he was practically invisible.'

'So, what kind of intruders was Jimmy afraid of, Sterling?'

'All sorts, Simon, but angry spirits mostly.'

'What kind of *angry spirits?*'

'The ghosts of all his victims more than likely. He must have slain thousands in his time. The ones that didn't survive to become vampires themselves probably turned into vengeful spirits, forever roaming the world in search of their killer.'

'You reckon we can gain entrance to the castle with all that voodoo attached to the place?'

'We should be all right. I doubt if he's hexed it against ordinary humans; or even vampires for that matter.'

'How can you tell?'

'Because if he had, I'd be throwing some kind of fit by now and you'd be stark raving mad, Simon. There, does that answer your question?'

The detective bit his lower lip. 'So, what are we going to do, Sterling?'

'I'm going in there?'

'What?' On your own?'

'Yes. I can't risk you getting lost inside that labyrinth. You'd never get out alive. Here, hold my bag for a moment. I'm going to check the place out. There's a network of spirit sensors covering the courtyard.'

'You sure? I can't see anything.'

'You can't see them because you don't have the vision, Simon. Believe me when I tell you this, but Silver's psychic defence system is second to none. It's like a gigantic spider's web out there.'

The detective frowned. 'You reckon it's safe?'

Sterling nodded and made to calm his fears. Then she gave a thumbs-up sign and began walking. Simon watched as she moved across the courtyard and made her way towards the inner bastion of the castle, stepping cautiously over the invisible threads of Silver's security system like she was in a James Bond movie. When he could no longer see her, he focused his thoughts back on the castle. His attention had been caught by the fleeting glimpse of someone's pale, lunar face looking down from a fourth floor window. Muttering an oath, he narrowed his gaze for a better view, but before he could refocus, the face was gone and the tall gothic window once more shuttered up against the night.

Had there really been a face at the window or had it been nothing more than an optical illusion? If not, then whose face had he seen? It sure wasn't Tamara's because it didn't have any hair. Who the hell could it have been?

He was about to hiss out a warning to his comrade when he saw her lithe silhouette emerge on the far side of the courtyard and make its way toward what he took to be the doors of an old coal cellar set at an angle in the base of the wall. He smiled when he saw her turn and give him another thumbs-up sign before yanking the padlock off the coal cellar doors with one sharp movement of her hands.

Then she was gone, swallowed up by the ancient castle. Whatever perils lay hidden within the confines of that forbidding fortress, she would have to face them alone. Simon was powerless to help her and he knew it.

16

Sterling lowered herself down, feeling for the floor of the cellar with the toe of her boot. Satisfied there actually was a floor to the place, she took a deep breath and paused to orientate herself. The cellar was dark and airless, but a slight breeze on her face told her that an exit point might be nearby.

Fighting a wave of nausea, she took a few cautious steps toward what she guessed might be a staircase leading up into the main body of the castle. Reaching the top of the stairs, she felt for the door. Good, it was unlocked.

The entrance hall was almost as dark as the cellar, its solid stone floor layered with centuries of dust. Whoever it was that lived here, they sure weren't too bothered about housekeeping. As she wandered through a series of interconnected rooms, her eyes slowly adjusted to the gloom, enabling her to gauge the overall feel of the place.

Christ, but it was eerie. Even to a creature like herself, the building was disturbing, with an austere, unwelcoming atmosphere which only intensified the further you went in. All this was compounded by the overall layout of the rooms with their weird, angular perspective whose sole purpose seemed to be one of leading the viewer's gaze beyond the normal field of vision and into realms of complete and total disorientation. She'd been right to leave Simon outside. No ordinary mortal could have withstood more than an hour's sustained exposure to a place like this without going completely insane. The whole castle was nothing more than a trap for the unwary mind. But why had it been built this way, she wondered?

Retracing her steps, she began climbing the wide baronial staircase that rose up from the central spine of the entrance hall. Judging by the thickness of the dust accumulated on its banister rails, she doubted if the castle had seen any visitors in a long time. Reaching the landing, she looked around, marvelling at the genius of whoever had designed the place.

There were a total of five floors in all, and for the most part, they were nearly all identical, the second floor being very much like the first, as was the third, fourth and fifth. The interior of the house was indeed as huge and labyrinthine as she'd feared, but that wasn't all. Apart from Tamara's presence, she could also feel the proximity of another, much more evil and malignant intelligence, hidden somewhere deep within the castle's massive walls and crazy rooms; but whether or not this additional presence was her old enemy, Jimmy Silver it was impossible to say. All she could hope for was that if this individual was indeed Silver, then he was either completely unaware of her intrusion, or at least powerless to track her down in the endless maze of staircases and gloomy corridors that formed the main body of the building.

As she left yet another sitting room with its peeling wallpaper and antique marble fireplace, she thought she glimpsed something small and pale reflected in one of the Venetian mirrors by the door. Turning to confront the apparition, she found she was looking at the ghost of a small girl-child who couldn't have been much more than five years of age at most.

Sterling knew the child to be a ghost because she was wearing the clothes of an earlier century and had a deep scar running across her neck where her throat had been cut. No living person could have survived a wound like that.

'Hello, young lady.'

The ghost-child blinked, clutching a small rag doll to its breast like it was the very last thing on earth.

'What's your name, little girl?'

The phantom smiled and extended a chubby hand in a gesture of friendship.

'Greta,' she replied with some difficulty. Whoever the child was, she clearly had no reason to trust an adult, but for some reason she trusted Sterling.

'Who killed you, Greta?'

'The peasants... a long time ago...'

Sterling guessed the child must have died in a popular uprising and continued with her questioning:

'Greta, do you know where I can find someone called, Tamara Sheridan?'

The ghost shook her head, 'No.'

'Is there anyone here who *does* know?'

The girl smiled again. 'Mummy knows.' Then she floated through the door and off down the corridor with Sterling in hot pursuit. Finally, the phantom apparition entered an oak-panelled room lined with bookshelves. There was a sudden rush of air followed by an icy chill and Sterling found herself standing face to face with another ghost.

'*Mutti,*' said the girl, floating over to where her mother stood, dressed in the clothes of a sixteenth-century German aristocrat, her hair the same colour as her daughter's but pulled back beneath a flat-topped circular hat worn at a jaunty angle on the head. The right side of her face had been smashed in and there was a huge, gaping wound in her stomach where someone had run her through with a hunting spear.

The ghost-child hugged her mother's skirt and pointed at Sterling. 'Look, Mother; the English lady has come.' At this moment, all the electric lights in the room suddenly flared up with a dazzling brilliance way beyond the range of an ordinary lightbulb.

'Were you the wife of Martin Karlsh?' asked Sterling, knowing full well what the answer might be.

The dead woman looked up, surprised that anyone should remember her husband's name.

'Frau, Karlsh, I need your help in finding an American lady who goes by the name of Tamara Sheridan. Do you know where she is?'

The ghost-woman looked down at her daughter and gestured for her to leave. The little girl instantly obeyed, rolling herself up into a tiny ball of energy and vanishing with a pop as Sterling looked on.

'Komm,' said the woman, motioning Sterling to follow her, whereupon she glided over to one of the oak panels set into the wall and passed clean through it as if it had never existed at all. Reasoning it must be a concealed door, Sterling searched until she found the secret catch that opened it. Then she went through and found the ghost waiting for her on the other side.

And then began the threading of a maze so labyrinthine as to suggest there was no end to it, as Sterling followed her spirit guide slowly through a series of dimly lit passageways until at length they came to a shorter corridor where the slanting section of yet another broader passageway led towards the landing of a narrow wooden staircase. Out of nowhere came the distant sound of a radio playing a contemporary pop song. It seemed to be coming from below and the ghost-woman indicated that Sterling should go downstairs.

Sterling nodded to show that she understood and began her downward climb. One, two, three levels of the secret staircase and the sound of the radio became louder. On reaching the fourth level, Sterling turned to look at the ghost. The phantom woman seemed terrified, and it was more than apparent that she would proceed no further down the staircase to whatever it was that lay below. Sterling nodded once more and continued on her way, wondering what on earth could be so bad down there to have frightened a ghost. Glancing back, she saw that the woman had disappeared, presumably having returned to care for her ghost-child and whatever solace they took in each other's company.

Reaching the bottom of the staircase, Sterling discovered yet another passageway leading off to the right. Following the sound of the radio, she walked on for a while until she came to a door. Unnerved at the prospect of whatever horrors might lie within, she hesitated for a moment before making her decision. Then she took a deep breath, grasped the handle and yanked the door open.

Another staircase.

Sterling shrugged and continued her descent down into the bowels of the castle. At the bottom of the stairs lay a small room whose only source of illumination was the pale blue light of a halogen heater. For some reason, the radio had stopped playing, leaving the atmosphere of the room still and close.

Then she saw her. It was Tamara Sheridan, lying drugged and unconscious on a bed, chained by her wrist to the bed frame. In the middle of the room was a table and two chairs. On the table was a rolled-up sheet of parchment, bound with a length of scarlet ribbon. Beside it was an old-fashioned inkpot, out of which protruded a quill pen made from a single white goose-feather. A folding screen stood in the corner next to an empty fireplace. Apart from this, there were no other items of furniture in the room.

Sterling walked over to the bed and regarded the young American as she lay there with her bright ginger hair splayed out across the pillow. She appeared to be unharmed and there were no signs of bite marks around her neck. Good. But what about the rest of her? What about the rumour that Jimmy Silver had wanted to sire a vampire super-child with her? Taking out her switchblade, Sterling passed it over Tamara's body. The blade glowed with a steady blue fluorescence, indicating the presence of something deep inside the woman's body. Something feral and alive.

'Damn it. Silver's got there first. I'm going to have to be quick.'

Hearing a sound, she tensed, turning her head just in time to see the vampire advancing slowly across the floor towards her. It must have been hiding behind the folding screen all the while she'd had her back turned. Now it growled out its challenge as it halted momentarily in its tracks waiting for her response. Grasping her switchblade, Sterling snarled and displayed her fangs to show she meant business. The other vampire mirrored this gesture and snarled back, making ready to charge. He was male, and judging from the type of clothing he was wearing, Sterling guessed he must have been one of the backpackers who'd recently been reported missing out in the Brocken forest and who must have made the mistake of coming to the castle in search of help. And yet, oddly enough, he was quite mature for all the short while he'd been a vampire. His rapidly extending fangs were well over an inch long and his eyes were the colour of claret wine just like her own. It had taken Sterling the better part of twenty years to evolve features like that, and yet this young man had managed to develop them in only a matter of weeks. Where had he sprung from, she wondered? He sure wasn't one of Jimmy Silver's creations, that much was certain. He was far too advanced for that.

Tamara stirred in her sleep as both vampires circled in the centre of the room, each sizing the other up before they clashed. Sterling could almost hear the cogs whirring in her opponent's brain as his brow furrowed. He was a young man and physically more powerful than she was, but he was also stupid, telegraphing the move he was about to make.

She stepped aside to dodge his charge, moving in beneath his reach to drive her knife into his side. The blade tore through the vampire's outer garment but failed to penetrate deeply enough to have any effect. The thick leather jacket he was wearing had seen to that. Not even a scratch!

Now he had her locked in a bear hug with both her arms pinned to her sides. She could feel his foul breath on her face as her bones began to bend in his vice-like grip. Still clutching her knife, she squirmed in an effort to work her arms free. This seemed to excite the young male vampire to the extent that she could feel his cock begin to harden as he became sexually aroused. Presumably, he was going to rape her before killing her.

She struggled again. Wrenching her arms free, she drove her switchblade hard into his right temple. It slid in smoothly, lobotomising him in an instant.

The vampire howled, dropping Sterling to the ground as it tried to pull the weapon out of its skull. Quickly, she assessed the damage to herself. Only a few cracked ribs. Good. Her opponent was not so lucky, however, crashing around the room and flailing his arms in the air before finally collapsing face downward on the floor, his cries halting in mid-flow.

Stepping cautiously towards the corpse, Sterling knelt down and retrieved her blade with a single twist. Then she riffled through the vampire's pockets in search of some clue as to its former identity. There was a brown leather wallet containing a few low-denomination banknotes and a driver's licence: Philip Ziegler. Born, 27 June 1996 and with a Munich address. Too bad. He wouldn't be going home.

Stuffing the banknotes into her own pocket, she wiped the blade clean on his shirt and folded it back into its sheath. It was then that she heard a woman's voice. The voice was weak and it was coming from the bed:

'The stairs, Sterling... He's coming down the stairs...'

Still squatting on her haunches, she turned to look. The body on the floor was beginning to decompose already, but that was the least of her problems compared to what it was that was now making its way down the staircase towards her with such slow and measured steps.

At first, she thought it was a castle goblin, one of the many strange creatures she'd learned about since becoming a vampire herself. It had the same pointed ears and clawed fingers that were characteristic of such beings, and its face was deathly pale with two vertical slits where its nose should have been; but whereas a castle sprite would most likely have sprung at her without a moment's hesitation, this thing just kept on walking down the stairway with all the poise and elegance usually reserved for senior members of the aristocracy. As it reached the bottom of the stairs, the creature turned its head slowly towards her and spoke her name.

'Good evening, Fraulein Sterling. It is indeed a pleasure to make your acquaintance at last. I've heard such a lot about you.'

It wasn't Jimmy Silver. For one thing, the creature looked a whole lot older than Silver, and for another, it spoke with an archaic German dialect that hadn't been voiced in centuries. No, whatever it was, it was obviously something far more ancient and malevolent than any type of vampire she had yet encountered.

'You are perplexed, Sterling?'

She stood up and slowly shook her head.

'Then you are afraid perhaps?'

Again, she shook her head. 'No, I'm not afraid.'

'Oh, really? You should be, you know. You really should be.'

She moved to put a bit of distance between herself and the malevolent being that was walking across the floor towards her. As it approached, it seemed to absorb all the energy in the room, causing the warm, blue glow of the halogen heater to become dimmer by the second. It was then that she realised what the creature was. The thing walking across the floor was a *duke*. She was standing face to face with one of the most senior vampires on the planet and what was more, she was on its own turf as well.

'My apologies for the mess,' it said nodding in the direction of the body on the carpet. 'He was expendable.'

'His name was Philip,' replied Sterling. 'I checked his wallet.'

'How interesting. I seldom bother to look any more.'

Sterling glanced momentarily at Tamara lying on the bed.

The American had passed out again; the effort of trying to warn her friend having been too much for her already weakened body.

'Let her lie,' said the ancient revenant. 'She needs to rest.'

'Why? What have you done to her?'

'I...? I have done nothing at all,' replied the duke, mildly amused by Sterling's accusation. 'What is it you think I have done?'

'Where's Jimmy Silver?' she replied without answering his question.

'Silver? He was staying as my guest here but had to leave on some urgent business or other. He said you might be coming and here you are. I must say, you look just like his description of you, mirrored sunglasses and all. I don't wear them myself. Seldom have the need. I spend most of my time asleep in this old castle of mine and only venture out whenever the mood takes me, *if you know what I mean.*'

The duke raised an eyebrow as if to emphasise the point. There wasn't much humanity left in the creature, who now more resembled the character Lord Voldemort from the Harry Potter stories than anything remotely human. Its clothes, too, looked at least a full century out of fashion; presumably dating back to the time it had last walked out of the Brocken forest and into the world of men. Evidently, this thing didn't need to hunt any more and probably just waited for its food to come willingly to its table by some form of telepathic suggestion. Leastways, that was the only explanation which made any sense or accounted for the dead backpacker lying there on the floor. It looked like Silver had set her up royally and there wasn't a damn thing she could do about it. The only question that remained was *why?* What did Silver have to gain by luring her here to this draughty old castle in the heart of Europe other than to seal her own destruction? But why go to all that trouble when all he had to do was just order a hit on her himself or wait until the Vatican did the job for him? It just didn't make sense.

'You're Leopold Kammler, aren't you?' she said at length, staring directly into his ebony black eyes.

'Bravo! Yes, I am Leopold Kammler... or rather, I was Kammler, but all that was a long time ago in a very different age. You should know about things like that, Sterling... or should I say, *Julie Kent.*'

'So, you know all about me then?'

'Indeed I do. It was Jimmy Silver who first brought you to my attention, though I was aware that something was amiss in England when one of my associates failed to return following a brief visit to your country back in 2003.'

'Who?'

'Baron von Geisenheim, of course. You must remember him, surely?'

'I do,' replied Sterling softly. 'Ulrich von Geisenheim was staying as a guest of Virginia Cavendish at her villa in Buckinghamshire.'

'Which was where he died?'

'Yes, but I didn't kill him. It was Virginia who did that.'

'But you did kill everyone else in the building, including Virginia herself and a not too insignificant number of the British establishment into the bargain. Nice touch that.'

'So, what? They all had it coming.'

Kammler smiled. 'My dear child, do not think that I am overly concerned about the death of Baron Ulrich. He was nothing more than a fop, a mere dilettante when compared to a master predator like yourself. You see, Sterling, I have been observing your murderous exploits for a good many years and can quite honestly say that I am greatly impressed by your abilities. You seem to possess a natural talent for mayhem and carnage that is second only to my own when I was your age. Oh, it needs refining of course — a few rough edges smoothed away — but believe me when I say this, that you have it within you to produce slaughter on a scale not witnessed since the days of Prince Vladimir if you try hard enough.'

'What are you saying, Kammler?'

'Saying?' the alpha vampire replied walking over to the table in the centre of the room. 'I am only offering you the chance of a lifetime, Sterling. Join with me like Silver did and you could have the whole world at your feet. Just think what you could become among the ranks of the Undead — a countess or even a marchesa perhaps, hmm? All you have to do is pick up this feather pen here and sign the document I've had drawn up. It's a contract binding you to me for two hundred years, after which time you are free to operate on your own. What do you say?'

'I came for the girl, Kammler; not a bloody job!'

'And you may have her, Sterling. She was never anything more than an excuse to lure you here anyway. I had Silver bait my trap well.'

'So, I can leave then, is that what you're saying?'

'Of course dear heart, but not before you have signed your contract of employment with me. After that, you are free to return to England with the girl, but you will be required to work for me from time to time just like Silver does. His contract runs out in six months' time, which is why I need a replacement like yourself to help run my business interests in

Europe. You didn't think Jimmy worked all on his own, did you?'

'Go to hell!'

Kammler frowned.

'Really, I'm surprised at you, Sterling. It's not every day that someone such as yourself gets an offer like this. Jimmy was around for well over a century before he came to work for me. How long has it been since you became what you are? Less than forty years from what I've heard, and in all that time you didn't think that your antics had gone unnoticed? How naïve of you.'

'I'm not signing a contract with you or anyone else, Kammler. I work on my own.'

The alpha vampire smiled, revealing a row of sharp, yellow fangs.

'Jimmy said you would be stubborn. I admire that quality in you, I really do, but you cannot deny me, Sterling. I have looked into your mind and I have glimpsed your fears. Silver was my creation and you are his granddaughter. You cannot kill me for the simple reason that I am part of you. Without me, you are nothing.'

'That remains to be seen.'

'Oh, come now, child. It would only further your interests if you were to join me. The world is changing fast. It's not our world any more. Humanity has reduced our race to a fairy tale; a lame excuse for a bad movie or a vampire novel. Think of the elegance and wit of our world, dear heart. It's all passing into history now, along with all the ghosts and goblins of our time. Nothing more than shadows on the wall of a crypt. Why, I can even remember when a lady would poison a duchess just to sit at the same table as a prince. Who would do that any more?'

'It sounds tempting, but no,' Sterling replied wryly. 'Now, why don't you shut the fuck up and let me go.'

The duke sighed and regarded the contract lying on the table next to the quill pen. 'You can't outrun the world, Sterling. Being a vampire isn't just about living forever. It's about living with yourself. You need me to help you do that.'

'Since when did you start running a counselling service, Leopold?'

'Ha! You remind me of dear Virginia when she was younger. Ever the one for dark humour she was. Now, why don't you sit with me at that table over there, pick up the pen and sign the contract? I'm sure you won't regret it.'

Sterling shook her head slowly. She sensed he was about to do something and steeled herself for whatever it might be. The atmosphere became tense as Kammler circled, never once taking his eyes from her. Already, the body on the floor was beginning to smoulder, filling the room in a haze of grey smoke. It wouldn't be long before it burst into flames making the air in the room unbreathable. Tamara would die.

'Yes, Sterling. There is still time. Sign the contract now and I will free your friend.'

'Never!' she yelled, following his circling movement with her gaze. Then she felt his mind lock onto hers with breathtaking speed, darting this way and that in an effort to gain access to what was left of her soul. It looked like he was going to make a psychic duel of it.

She moaned as his dark will flowed around her own like a giant python squeezing its prey. God, but he was powerful, she thought. More powerful than Jimmy Silver had been the last time they'd clashed. She seriously doubted she would be able to resist the elder vampire in the same way she'd managed to deal with Silver. Back then, she'd had the support of Joe Rackham and his gang of Hell's Angels to come to her rescue. Out here in the middle of nowhere, she had nothing. She was on her own.

Tamara stirred in her drug-induced coma, causing Kammler to become momentarily distracted. Seizing her advantage, Sterling reached for the switchblade in her pocket only to find herself thrown backwards across the room and pinned to the wall by the duke's telekinetic power. She hadn't reckoned on this aspect of his being and pretty soon she discovered he had another weapon at his command.

Resistance is futile, she heard him say. *You cannot deny me.*

His telepathic voice filled her mind until she thought it would burst. He was taking her over bit by bit; accessing all her memories and using them against her.

Thinking of running, dear heart?

'Get out of my head, Kammler! Get out of my fucking head!!'

'I will in due course, my sweetness, but I'm finding it too entertaining at the moment. Did you really cut that young man's nose off in that bar in Soho?'

'Fuck off!'

'Oh, and now we come to the bit where you destroyed Virginia Cavendish and all her cronies at that party in Buckinghamshire. Now, that was a slaying to be proud of. A veritable work of art, if I may say so myself.'

She realised that Kammler was now witnessing everything she had seen and done over her lifetime of being a vampire. He saw scenes of violence that would have shocked even the most hardened forensic pathologist, so intense were the images that passed before his mind's eye. In some, the hapless victims were seen trying to make a run for it before Sterling closed in for the kill. The screaming was the worst part, but it usually didn't last long before each individual was quickly despatched and drained of their blood with ruthless mechanical efficiency. Yet more examples of her handiwork followed in quick succession, each more cunning and brutal than the last until at length they all flowed into one monstrous tableaux of homicide that would have rendered every serial killer and professional hitman on the planet green with envy. It was only when Kammler came to the episode of Sterling's meeting with Lucifer that he withdrew his psychic hold and allowed her some respite in the proceedings. That he was genuinely surprised by this revelation was evident in the expression on his face, but Sterling was in no fit state to argue, so drained was she by the effect of his assault on her mind.

'All right, all right,' she exclaimed, sliding down the wall as the arch-fiend relaxed his telekinetic grip. 'I'll sign your damn contract. Just get the fuck out of my head!'

She's one of Lucifer's brood, murmured Kammler to himself. His expression had reverted to a thin smile, but he wasn't happy. Dealing with an underling like Sterling was one thing, but crossing swords with Lucifer was quite another. He would have to be vigilant.

'Good,' he said at length, indicating she make herself comfortable at the table. 'Please be seated and read the document carefully. When you have finished, you may sign it in red ink with the quill pen I have provided.'

'I prefer to use my own pen,' replied Sterling dryly.

'Very well, but be quick about it. That body on the floor

is beginning to stink. Come, sit yourself down and review our agreement. I'm sure you will find many things in it to your liking.'

Kammler watched as Sterling sat down and unscrolled the contract, smoothing it out on the table with her hands. Then he lit a tall candle in a pewter holder and brought it across so she could see more clearly by its light. 'For the small print,' he said seating himself down in the opposite chair. 'We wouldn't want you to miss anything, would we?'

Quietly, she ignored him and continued reading down the page. Kammler's penmanship was exquisite. Clearly, he had been a highly educated individual in his time; either that, or he had his own personal legal secretary hidden captive somewhere else in the building. As the moments passed by, the smoke from the body on the floor thickened, causing her to cough and splutter occasionally as she read on. Once she'd finished reading, Sterling glanced up, regarding the duke from behind her mirrored sunglasses:

'Well, everything appears to be in order, Kammler. Where do I sign?'

The duke looked surprised.

'So soon? Do you not wish to examine the document more thoroughly, Sterling?'

'No. I reckon I've seen enough,' she replied reaching into her jacket pocket. Kammler flinched in his seat anticipating a weapon. Instead, she pulled out a sleek, black fountain pen and began fiddling with its top. 'My pen,' she said, tilting her head to one side. 'I hope you don't mind?'

'Be my guest,' the duke responded, not suspecting anything untoward. It was only when he saw the open barrel of the pen pointing directly at his chest that he became concerned.

Too late!

With a single movement of her fingers, Sterling twisted the pen top and pushed it in, firing the weapon at point-blank range. A single .22 calibre bullet slammed into the duke, knocking him backwards in his chair and onto the floor. He sprawled for a few seconds clutching at his chest and growling expletives into the air. Then he tried to rise up, but it was no good. The toxins from the silver bullet were already spreading through his system, destroying every nerve ending in his body and reducing his capillary blood vessels to a mushy pulp.

'You damn English bitch!' he screamed. 'You fucking damn English bitch!! You'll never find your way out of here alive. There's no way out of this castle without my guidance.'

Sterling smiled. 'Thanks, Kammler, but I'm afraid you've got a couple of traitors in your midst.'

'Who?' the duke gasped, grabbing the edge of the table with his long, bony fingers, the claws scratching deep furrows in the wood as he struggled to gain what purchase he could.

'Your two resident ghosts, of course — Frau Karlsh and her daughter; or had you forgotten all about them, hmm?'

And so it went on; the classic Hollywood vampire scene as Kammler struggled for life on the floor. How he roared and screeched like a steam whistle, flailing his arms about in distress until at length a steady blue flame emerged from the centre of his chest and began consuming him alive in its sacred fire. When at length he could fight it no longer, Kammler raised himself up on one elbow and snarled out his final curse:

'Don't look so smug, Sterling. You're not unique. One day, Cardinal de Valois will die and you will lose his protection. Then the Church will hunt you down and seal your fate just like all the rest of us.'

'I reckon I can live with it, Leopold. My only mission here is to rescue Tamara from whatever it is that you and Silver did to her.'

He died quicker than the other vampire who'd been much younger; so much so that within less than a minute, all that remained of Leopold Kammler was a stark black shape on the floor and the sticky remains of his body fat as it sank slowly into the carpet.

'Good old, Liu,' said Sterling as she pocketed the gun pen. 'There's nothing like an ancient Chinese doctor when you need one.'

Picking up the contract, she rolled it up and touched it to the candle flame until it began to smoulder. Watching it burn, she turned to Tamara. The young American was beginning to stir once more, the effect of the drug having worn off and the sound of Kammler's dying oaths having roused her from her sleep.

'I've been raped,' was all Tamara said as she coughed and gagged in the smoky atmosphere.

'So have I,' replied Sterling, yanking hard on the chain securing Tamara to the bed until it snapped. 'Now, let's get the fuck out of here before the whole place goes up in smoke!'

***

'Thank you,' said Sterling to the lady ghost as they stood on the front porch of the castle. 'We couldn't have found our way out of there without your help. The flames from Kammler's body will quickly consume the castle setting both you and your daughter's spirits free. You won't feel a thing, I can guarantee it.'

'Danke, gut,' hissed the ghost of Frau Karlsh in reply, placing a phantom hand on her daughter's shoulder. 'Now we shall both be at rest. Thank you, Sterling. Thank you for everything.'

As the apparition slowly faded away, Sterling took Tamara by the wrist and walked briskly across the courtyard to where Simon was waiting beneath the ivy-festooned archway in the castle's outer wall. A thin sliver of light showed in the eastern sky telling her that it was dawn.

'What kept you?' he exclaimed, rubbing his hands together in the morning chill.

'It's a long story, Simon. Try watching the movie *Night of the Living Dead* and you'll get the gist of it. Oh, and this is Tamara by the way. She's been absolutely *dying* to meet you. Now, let's get ourselves back to Wernigerode pronto and catch the next fucking plane out of Germany. I've got a feeling this is not over yet.'

17

Simon sat on the balcony of their hotel bedroom holding a glass of schnapps in his hand while everything he had ever assumed was real disintegrated around him.

Had he really visited a demon's lair with a vampire called Sterling? Had they actually been attacked by a werewolf in the middle of an enchanted wood? And had they just burned a famous historical landmark to the ground? Well, yes, they had, and now he was trying to piece together all the events of the night before in his mind.

He took another swallow of his drink and glanced over the rim at Sterling. She was sitting on the bed with Tamara and they were both talking. He couldn't make out much of what they were saying apart from the odd word or phrase, but it was when Sterling mentioned the word "abortion" and drew out her switchblade that he became concerned. So did Tamara, backing herself up against the headboard of the bed and drawing her knees up to her chest in a defensive posture.

'Lie down,' said Sterling softly, laying a reassuring hand on Tamara's shoulder. The American girl shook her head and backed off further.

'I'm not going to hurt you, Tamara. I just want to pass this knife over your belly, that's all. Pull up your shirt and vest, and lie flat on the bed. Do it now…'

She's using a telepathic command, thought Simon. *What the fuck is she up to now?*

He watched as Tamara lay down on the duvet allowing Sterling to unclasp her blade and pass the knife slowly over her stomach several times. As she did so, Simon saw the cold metallic surface of the weapon give off a milky blue fluorescence until the glow from the steel filled the confines of the room with an eerie haze.

'Thought so,' said his friend at last. 'You're pregnant.'

'I am?' replied Tamara coming out of her trance and sitting up on the bed.

'Yes, and you're carrying an incubus inside you as well.'

'A what?'

'A baby demon, Tamara; and it's most likely Kammler's if I'm not very much mistaken.'

'No it's not.'

'What do you mean?' said Sterling regarding Tamara strangely.

'There was another man in the building a short while before you arrived. Kammler kept referring to him as Jimmy. It was him who raped me.'

Sterling creased her brow and sighed. 'That figures. Well, it doesn't matter anyway. That vampire child you're carrying has got to come out of your belly pronto on the orders of the Vatican.'

'No way! You're not using that knife on me. If I've got to have an abortion, I'm having it done in a hospital like everyone else.'

'Don't worry, Tamara. There won't be any need for surgery. Just a little medication, that's all.'

'A drug?'

'Yes. I was given something by this Chinese doctor I know. It's called the Herb of Grace. Works like a charm apparently.'

Sterling reached across the bed and removed a small paper bag from out of her brown leather satchel. Then she picked up the electric kettle from the bedside table and wandered off into the bathroom to fill it with water. While she was gone, Simon got up from his chair and came into the room, sitting himself down on the edge of the bed beside Tamara.

'Everything's going to be fine,' he said, comforting the girl. 'We'll get you out of this mess, you'll see.'

'You sure about that?' Tamara replied, gesturing with her eyes in the direction of the bathroom.

'Oh, don't worry about, Sterling. She's on our side.'

'But she's one of *them,* Simon.'

'Yes, but she works for the Vatican.'

'The *Vatican?*'

'Yeah. Under the direction of some cardinal or other. She told me all about it.'

'And you believe her?'

'I've no reason not to. Up until a few days ago, I didn't believe in any of this, but recent events have proved me wrong. Now, shut up. Here she comes with your brew.'

Sterling walked into the room and clicked the electric kettle on at the switch. Then she emptied the dried herbs out from the paper bag into a cup and waited for the kettle to boil. Once it had boiled, she poured the steaming hot water over the herbs and allowed them to percolate for a few moments before offering the cup to Tamara. 'Here, drink this,' she said. 'It takes a while to work but it's very effective in terminating early pregnancies. At least that's what ten million Chinese think.'

***

'How is she?'

Tamara had been in the bathroom for well over an hour and Simon was beginning to get concerned.

'She's bleeding quite heavily,' answered Sterling who had just re-entered the room. 'Don't worry. It's not enough to kill her. She just needs to rest, that's all.'

'You sure that Chinese doctor knew what he was doing giving you those herbs?'

'Yeah. Like I said, she just needs to rest. Now, get a move on and pour me that drink I asked for.'

As Simon went over to the minibar, Sterling checked her pockets and counted out the money she was carrying. Good, there'd be enough for another day's expenses but not much more. That would give Tamara time to recover and then they could check out of the hotel and make their way back to England.

'Here's your drink, Sterling. Jack Daniel's, like you said. I poured myself one as well.'

'Have as many as you like, Simon. We're not paying for them.'

'Eh?'

'We're not paying for them. We leave early tomorrow morning without settling up. We need to keep our money for the return journey. How much have you got on you, by the way?'

'About five hundred Euros, Sterling. Is that okay?'

'It should be enough with what I've got. Otherwise, we're hitching it, and I don't think Tamara is in a fit enough state for that yet.'

Simon was just about to ask what method of transport they

would be using when there was a knock on the door. It was a rhythmic, cryptic sort of a knock and it caused Sterling to turn her head sharply as if she recognised the sound.

'Who's that?' she exclaimed with a look of concern, gesturing Simon to hide in the bathroom in case there was trouble.

'Sterling... is that you?' came a muffled voice from beyond the door.

'Joe...?'

'Yes, it's me. And I've got Skinner with me too. Open the door. We haven't got very much time.'

Sterling opened the door and found Joe Rackham and Jerry Skinner standing outside in the corridor. They both looked concerned.

'You'd better come in,' she said with a sideways jerk of her head. 'Sit down and I'll get you boys a drink. You both look like you could do with one.'

'Ta,' replied Joe sitting himself down in a low armchair beside the bed. Jerry frowned and went over to the balcony window, glancing down into the street below. It's all clear, Joe. Everything is sweet out there.'

Joe nodded and leaned forward in his chair to accept a glass of Jack Daniel's from Sterling. 'Ah-h-h, that's better,' he exclaimed, downing the whisky in a single gulp. 'I needed that.'

'So, what's up, Joe? How come you knew we were here?'

Joe leaned forward once again and allowed Sterling to pour him another shot of whisky. 'Well, Sterl, it was like this. I was sitting at home watching telly with the missus when the phone rings in the kitchen. Sheila goes to answer it and comes back into the room saying as how she's got some bloke on the other end of the line and he's not making much sense.'

'And who was it?'

'David fucking Kessler, that's who it was, and he was well pissed off.'

'Oh, really; and why might that be, Joe?'

'Maybe you can tell me, Sterling. He seemed to know an awful lot about you.'

'I can't think why. I mean, what would he be angry at me for?'

'He was angry on account of you having nailed his hand to a nightclub table, that's what!'

'Oh — that.'

'Yes, *that*. And what's more, he was screaming blue murder down the phone at me to the effect that if he ever caught up with you, you'd be in Hell before the Devil knew you were dead!'

'Would that be a problem, Joe? I mean, I'm not exactly a stranger to the infernal regions as you well know.'

'Not funny, Sterling. Anyway, our main problem now is in getting you and Tamara out of this town as soon as possible.'

'Why?'

'Because, Kessler's probably mobilised every Hell's Angel gang in the Netherlands by now and they're all out looking for you, that's why.'

'But, Tamara's in no fit state to travel yet. We were thinking of leaving early tomorrow morning and—'

Just then, the bathroom door opened and Simon emerged from hiding, along with Tamara following meekly behind. 'She's okay,' he said. 'Just a bit weak, that's all. If we've got to get out of here then we do it now, just like Joe says.'

'Yes,' added Skinner returning from the window. 'Collect

your things and follow us out of the hotel one at a time with three-minute intervals between each of you. That way, you won't be spotted leaving as a group. We'll all meet up in the town square in about twenty minutes time. Joe's got a white campervan parked up a side road near there. There'll be a couple of Joe's mates with their motorcycles standing nearby. They're both Hell's Angels from Essex with long hair and pushing fifty. Their names are Spike and Gordon. You can't miss them.'

'Just one thing,' said Sterling as she went to collect her bag. 'How come you knew where we were, Joe?'

'Huh?'

'How did you know where to find us? I mean, Germany is a big place after all.'

'Simple,' replied Joe. 'Kessler let on you were staying in Wernigerode. Once we got here, we just kept asking around all the hotels in town until we found this one. Now, grab your stuff and follow us out. We've got a long journey ahead of us back to London and I've a feeling it's not going to be an easy one, what with Kessler's mob on the warpath as well.'

18

'Good idea of yours to follow the country roads, Joe.'

'I guess so, Sterl, but we'll have to join the autobahn sooner or later. I'm not familiar with this part of Europe and the German motorway system is the most direct route west.'

'I still don't see what was so bad about my idea of taking a plane,' put in Simon who was sitting in the back of the van with Tamara. 'We could have been back in London inside of three hours instead of having a grand tour of the Fatherland.'

'Too dangerous,' replied the old biker. 'Kessler's boys will be watching all the terminals. In any case, the nearest airport is Hanover and that's over one hundred kilometres to the north from here. We need to keep south to stand any chance of giving Kessler the slip. Best way is to stick to the back roads until we get clear of the Belgian border. Then we can make a dash for it on to the autobahn. This thing I'm driving is pretty nippy for a campervan.'

'It had better be,' remarked Skinner, sitting in the front passenger seat wedged in between Sterling and Joe who was driving. 'The way those Krauts drive over here is enough to put you off driving for life—'

'Uh-h-h-h-h...'

'You okay, Tamara?' exclaimed Sterling, turning round in her seat to see the American girl hunched over in the backseat of the van clutching at her stomach.

'No-o-o-o-oh; I've got a pain in my guts and I feel sick.'

'It's stomach cramps, kid. You've just shat out a fifth level incubus — what do you expect?'

'But it hurts, Sterling. It *h-u-u-urts.*'

'Well, we can't stop now. Here, have a Trebor mint. It'll help settle your stomach.'

'No. I think I'm going to be sick. Pull over and let me out... *ple-e-e-ease.*'

Simon nodded. 'Best stop the van, Joe. I think she means it.'

'All right, but don't take long. I'm not at all sure where the fuck we are.'

As Tamara heaved and retched by the side of the road, Sterling turned to Skinner with a puzzled look on her face. 'Where exactly are we, Jerry?' she exclaimed, jabbing a finger at the road map on his knee.

'About ten kilometres outside of Lutherstadt. Why do you ask?'

'I ask because that sign back there clearly said: "You are now entering Thuringia. Please drive carefully," that's why.'

'We can't be—'

'But we are, Jerry. We *are.*'

'Hmm, let's see... We left Wernigerode about six hours ago heading west, then we turned south into...'

'We turned south into the Thuringian Forest, Jerry. Thanks to your navigation skills we've ended up in the middle of a national park.'

'Well, Joe said we had to head south, so I guess we're okay, ain't that right Joe?'

'Uh...? What's that you say?'

Joe wasn't listening. He was too busy looking in the rear-view mirror and taking occasional glances over his shoulder to pay any heed to the conversation now in progress.

'I said, you wanted us to keep travelling south to avoid Kessler's men, didn't you?'

'Oh, yeah — I did. Why, what's the problem?'

'Jerry's gone and landed us in the middle of Thuringia, miles away from anywhere,' cut in Sterling. 'That's the problem.'

'Keep your head down kid,' was all Joe said in reply as he glanced in the mirror. 'I think we've got visitors.'

'What?'

'I said, keep your head down, Sterl. There's a column of bikers coming up the road behind us and I think they're Hell's Angels.'

The roar of engines grew louder then faded as a posse of ten or more motorcyclists drove by, all apparently oblivious to the white campervan parked up by the side of the road.

'They didn't spot us,' exclaimed Jerry emerging from behind his road map.

'Yeah, but they were Kessler's men all right,' answered Joe. 'I clocked the insignia on the back of their jackets. They're a Netherlands chapter from Rotterdam.'

'So what are we going to do?' queried Simon as he helped Tamara back into the van.

'We wait here until Spike and Gordon show up. I think we lost them when we crossed that autobahn earlier on.'

'That's assuming they haven't had a run-in with that Rotterdam chapter and legged it,' added Sterling sucking on a mint.

'I don't think so,' added Joe, tapping a fingernail on his rear-view mirror. 'Here they come now.'

Sterling rolled down her side window as the two bikers

pulled up alongside the van and stopped. 'You okay, Spike?' she yelled above the sound of their engine noise.

'Sure,' replied the man on the first bike, removing his helmet to reveal a shock of matted grey hair. The other man kept his helmet on and remained silent throughout the exchange.

'Did you see those Dutch guys who just went through?' continued Jerry, gesturing up the road with a nod of his head.

'Uh-huh, there were twelve of them,' replied Spike. 'We gave them the slip about five miles back. Gordon reckons they're packing.'

'How about you?'

'I'm unarmed, but Gordon's got a Glock 17. He picked it up when we came through Belgium.'

'Well, just make sure you chuck it before we get to Calais,' put in Joe leaning across the front seat. 'We don't want to get caught with a gun on us at the customs barrier.'

The silent man nodded and gave a salute with two closed fingers to the side of his helmet to show he understood.

'So, what's the plan?' continued Spike, looking at Sterling. 'How do we get the cargo through Germany to the English Channel without having to make a fight of it?'

'The *cargo,* as you put it, is a girl called Tamara, and she's just had an abortion in case you didn't realise it.'

'I'm all right,' came a tremulous voice from the back of the van. 'Just a little queasy, that's all.'

Spike glanced at Tamara with a puzzled expression on his face. Then he looked at Jerry: 'Let's see the map,' he exclaimed with a note of resignation in his voice. He'd been involved in some of Sterling's capers before and knew from bitter experience just how bad things could get.

Joe climbed out of the van and wandered over to where Spike was standing with Sterling who had also left the vehicle and was now engaged in a heated debate with Spike as to the best route they should take to ensure they all reached Calais in one piece. The man with the gun just stood beside his motorcycle glancing up the road. He'd said nothing in all the while they'd been talking and he was beginning to give Simon the creeps. If anything kicked off over the next few hours then this was the guy who was going to settle the score.

'There's nothing else for it,' declared Sterling, jabbing a finger at the map. 'We'll carry on driving south until we reach Schweinfurt then head northwards up into Hesse.'

'Won't that mean having to use the autobahns?' observed Spike, tracing a line up from Schweinfurt to the town of Marburg and then on to Cologne.

'Yes it will, but what other option do we have? It's the quickest way to the Belgian frontier, assuming we want to get into France and travel down to Dunkirk and Calais using the coast road.'

'What happens when we get to Calais?' enquired Joe, rubbing a three-day-old growth of chin stubble with his thumb and forefinger.

'We split up. I travel with you, Jerry, Simon and Tamara in the van through the Channel Tunnel to Dover, while Spike and Gordon take their bikes over on the ferry. That way, we won't draw attention to ourselves and I won't get a crushing migraine attack on account of having to cross a large body of water. You know what we vampires are like with water.'

'What about the American girl? Has she got all the right papers?'

'I very much doubt it. She was bundled out of England

under duress, so I doubt if she had time to grab her passport.'

'So, what do we do if she gets pulled?'

'I'll just have to turn the customs official if we get stopped. It shouldn't be a problem once I get inside his mind.'

'Careful you don't fry his brains, Sterl. You know what happened the last time.'

The vampire beamed a cheeky grin and ran her tongue along the edge of her top lip. 'Don't worry, Joe. I prefer to leave them sane these days.'

'Must be getting soft in your old age then,' muttered the old biker climbing back into his van. 'Okay you lot, let's roll,' he said making the panzer sign with his fist at Spike and Gordon. 'We've got a long journey ahead of us and I think the weather's closing in. We'll be lucky to reach Belgium by nightfall at this rate.'

***

'I can smell the sea.'

It was Jerry who spoke, and he was right. A thin sliver of early morning sunlight revealed the otherwise grey expanse of the English Channel beyond the low hills and hedgerows that fringed either side of the coastal route leading down to Dunkirk and Calais.

'We made it,' exclaimed Simon, squinting bleary-eyed out of the campervan's nearside window at the maritime horizon.

'Where are we?' enquired Tamara, rising up from the narrow sofa-bed beside the van's rudimentary kitchen.

'Just beyond the Franco-Belgian border,' replied Sterling answering the girl's question. 'You slept through the entire night.'

'I did?'

'Yes — you needed it as well, kid. I was beginning to get worried about you.'

'I'm okay now... *I think*. I had some pretty scary dreams though.'

'You would. Getting yourself impregnated by an alpha vampire isn't something that happens to a girl every day.'

'I'm hungry. Can we stop for breakfast?'

'Good idea, Tamara,' put in Joe. 'I've been driving for well over twelve hours. I need to pull in.'

'But we're nearly there,' complained Sterling. 'The ferry terminal is just another thirty miles down the road.'

'No, I need to stop. What harm will it do, look — there's a service station up ahead. Let's get ourselves a coffee and a bite to eat.'

The service station was practically deserted, but the mood around the table was jolly as the seven weary travellers made short work of demolishing a full English breakfast washed down with generous servings of coffee and thick, buttered toast.

'I could do with that all over again,' exclaimed Joe, pushing aside his plate and pouring out his third coffee of the hour. It was still quite early in the day and the restaurant had yet to fill up with its usual crowd of truck drivers and tourists.

'Make sure you go to the bog before we set off again,' said Jerry mopping up some egg yolk from his plate with the remains of his toast. 'You won't be able to go once we're in the Tunnel.'

Joe nodded and continued with his long-established ritual of emptying two sachets of brown sugar into his coffee mug while craftily pocketing a third for some obscure moment in the future that never actually came. No one knew exactly why he did this — he just did, and nobody thought to question it. Joe was a law unto himself.

'Just nipping out for a ciggie,' declared Spike getting up from his chair. Gordon joined him, and both men wandered out of the restaurant leaving the others sitting around the table near the window finishing off their meal. Outside, the weather was turning grey and overcast after a promising start to the day.

'Looks like rain,' observed Simon glancing up at the sky above the station forecourt.

'Yeah, well we ain't got much further to go,' replied Joe pocketing yet another bag of sugar. 'I'll be glad when we get onto a proper British motorway. These continental roads are bleedin' murder.'

Beyond the window, Spike and Gordon could be seen talking together beneath the pedestrian awning. As Spike turned up the collar of his jacket against the chill, a group of three motorcyclists pulled in at the petrol stop across the forecourt and dismounted from their machines. One of the riders glanced momentarily at Spike then turned to his two associates, gesturing with a nod of his head in Spike's direction.

'Joe?'

It was Jerry who spoke, nudging Joe Rackham on the elbow.

'Uh-huh,' grunted the old biker without making eye contact. He was too busy hand-rolling a cigarette to take any notice of what Jerry had to say.

'Out of the window, Joe...'

Joe looked and Sterling followed the direction of his gaze. Things were now developing fast out there on the forecourt as five more bikers arrived and parked their machines around the petrol pumps. Slowly, Spike and Gordon edged themselves away from the window trying not to attract any more attention than they possibly could. Gordon entered the restaurant first and walked over to have a quiet word with Joe.

'There's fucking loads of 'em boss and they're all tooled up an' all.'

'Who?' exclaimed Joe, turning to look at Gordon.

'Kessler and his mates, that's who. I recognise his bike. Big Harley Davidson low-rider with customised twin exhausts. I've seen it in a biker magazine. It's him.'

'You certain?'

'No mistake, boss,' said Gordon reaching for his gun. 'It's Kessler all right, and there's another four of them coming up the slip road. What do I do?'

'Well, you can take your hand off that barker of yours for starters. This is a public area in case you hadn't noticed. There'll be security cameras.'

Gordon looked around the room then slipped a glance at Sterling for reassurance.

'Joe's right,' she declared. 'We'd be better off trying to make a run for it before this place starts filling up. You go with Spike and create a diversion while I take Tamara out the back way with Simon and the others. Then we'll come round to where Joe parked the van and head for Calais.'

Gordon nodded and looked to Spike. 'What about me using the shooter on them once we're clear of this place?'

Spike frowned and looked to Sterling for an answer. 'You'd best hand me that pistol,' she replied. 'I don't think we need to be attracting any more attention than is reasonably necessary. In any case, you both stand a better chance of outpacing Kessler's men on those bikes of yours than we would in Joe's van.'

Reluctantly, Gordon took the gun from his inside pocket and slid it across the table towards Sterling. 'It was only a shoot 'n' chuck anyway,' he growled. 'Careful you don't blow your hand off.'

'I won't,' replied the vampire pocketing the weapon. 'Now, if there's nothing else you wish to discuss, then I suggest we best be on our way and put our plan into action. You and Spike take off on your bikes and make it obvious that you're doing a runner. Head off down the slip road at normal speed then accelerate rapidly just before you reach the motorway. That should draw Kessler's attention long enough for us to reach the van undetected. Then, while you're being chased, we'll drive off in the direction of Calais and wait for you there.'

'I see,' said Spike. 'So we outrun them for a few miles then cross the central reservation and double back?'

'I'll leave the details up to you, Spike. Just make it look convincing, that's all. If we don't join up in Calais, I'll square everything up with you once we get back to England. Agreed?'

Spike nodded and cast a glance at Joe who indicated his agreement by raising a forefinger. 'Sterling's on the level, Spike. In any case, I don't see any way out of this mess other than by doing exactly what she says. I only hope Tamara's old man is as good as his word with Simon here and we get cut in on the deal. I've got a horrible feeling we're all about to deserve it.'

***

'You're a fucking Jonah you are, Sterl!'

It was Joe and he was pissed off. Even with the sole of his boot pressed down hard on the accelerator, he still wasn't putting much distance between himself and the gang of Hell's Angels who were rapidly bearing down on him in the fast lane and about to force him off the road.

'Well, how was I to know they were going to split up?' replied the vampire glancing out of the rear window at the approaching column of motorcycles.

'Yeah, well they did, and it's Kessler who's leading them,' added Jerry Skinner biting his lower lip. 'Come on, Joe — give her all you've got.'

'I couldn't get any more out of this crate if I got out and pushed,' growled Joe. 'Old campervans aren't built for speed.'

'What are we going to do?' queried Simon anxiously. 'Kessler's flashing his heads. I think he wants us to pull over.'

'Well, he can fuck off. There's a turn-off up ahead. Maybe I can lose them in one of the sideroads.'

'You're the driver, Joe. Do whatever you think fit.'

'Okay, hold on everybody—'

Everyone lurched sideways as Joe swung the campervan into a handbrake turn and headed off up a narrow access road that led in the direction of what looked like a small industrial estate. Just as he predicted, the gang chasing him overshot the junction and carried on down the road unable to take the turn without catapulting themselves off their bikes and into the coarse hedgerows and shrubbery that lined the edge of the hard shoulder.

'That's done for 'em,' he chuckled as he fought to keep the campervan under control. 'I didn't think the old girl had it in her.'

'Just keep driving,' said Jerry. 'We need to hide this crate somewhere and wait until nightfall. It's the only way we stand any chance of getting out of this alive.'

'I've got Gordon's pistol,' put in Sterling. 'That should even things up a bit.'

'Depends on what they're packing,' interrupted the American girl, her voice becoming suddenly stronger. 'That guy, Spike said they were armed.'

'They usually are, Tamara. Don't worry; we should be okay once we get among those huts over there. I think there's some people around. Those Dutch bikers won't try anything with people around.'

'I don't think so,' was all Tamara said in reply as the van sped on towards the collection of ramshakled huts and tumbledown dwellings that formed the makeshift village up ahead. Piles of rubbish and discarded tents lay scattered about and several campfires were still burning in the early morning air as a few people, mostly teenagers and young adults, wandered aimlessly around with little else to do but stare vacantly at the white campervan as it approached down the tarmac lane.

'What is this place?' exclaimed Simon as they drove slowly through the squatters village looking for somewhere to hide.

'I don't know,' replied Tamara warily. 'It sure doesn't look like an industrial estate to me. It's more like a refugee camp than anything else.'

'I think I know what it is,' piped up Jerry Skinner. 'I reckon it's one of those migrant camps they keep talking about in the news.'

'I thought they'd closed them all down,' remarked Joe as

he brought the van to a halt outside a small, single storey utility building which seemed to function as the camp's only latrine.

'They did, but that didn't stem the flow of refugees,' Jerry continued. 'There aren't as many of them as there used to be but they still keep coming. They're Afghans and Syrians mostly, but there's also a few from North Africa and the Yemen.'

'Why are they here?' asked Tamara whose voice appeared to be getting stronger by the minute.

'Civil war and job prospects mostly,' answered Jerry casually. 'Some just come because they've heard they can have a better life in England, though Christ knows why anyone should think that.'

'Why don't they just stay in France?'

'Dunno. I've heard quite a few of them have already got relatives living in the UK, so I suppose it makes it easier for them to claim asylum once they land in Dover.'

'And they can do that, can they?'

'Yes, they can. Anyway, here comes one of them now. Maybe you can ask him yourself.'

Tamara looked out of the window and watched as a young man wearing jeans, brown trainers and a hoodie walked towards the campervan and stood staring in at the occupants inside.

'What the fuck does he want?' exclaimed Joe irritably.

'Who knows? Maybe he's hungry,' answered Sterling, rolling down the passenger-side window.

'Yeah, well we ain't got any food, tell him.'

'He doesn't want food, Joe…'

'Well, what does he want then?' replied the biker marvelling at Sterling's mastery of foreign languages.

'He wants us to smuggle him across the Channel into England, that's what he wants. He says his name is Ahmed and he's got relatives living in Luton.'

'Well he can fuck off. We haven't come all this way just to get ourselves copped by the border police.'

Sterling shook her head at the young man and he wandered off looking dejected. He couldn't have been more than seventeen years of age but he looked much older.

'It's a pity we couldn't take him,' remarked Jerry. 'He looked pretty desperate.'

'They're all pretty desperate,' replied Joe. 'Take one and we'd have to take them all. We haven't got room in the van.' He was about to add words to the effect that maybe they could return at some future date with a larger van when the sound of motorcycle engines cut him short.

'Shit! It's Kessler's mob — they're back!'

Simon turned to look out of the window in the direction of the noise. 'There's five of them,' he exclaimed. 'What are we going to do?'

'You guys stay in the van,' declared Sterling opening the side passenger door. 'Kessler's not after you lot. It's me he wants.'

'Sterling!'

Too late. She was off, scampering across the waste ground in the direction of a series of outbuildings that looked like the remains of an abandoned dairy farm, complete with its milking parlour and cattle sheds.

'Stupid bitch,' seethed Joe banging the palm of his hand down on the steering wheel. 'She's going to get herself killed.'

'How the hell can she do that?' Skinner declared. 'She's already dead.'

'You know what I mean. The way them vampires have got of dealing with one another if they don't get on. She'll go up in smoke. I've seen it happen before.'

'So have I,' muttered Simon. 'So have I…'

'But she's got a gun,' Jerry went on, 'and it's a Glock 17 as well.'

'It's not enough,' replied Joe. 'She's got no silver bullets in the magazine. Unless she can get a head shot in, she's finished.'

'You reckon that's what she's up to then? Leading Kessler off the scent until she can get a pop at him in the napper?'

'It's likely, unless she's got something else up her sleeve. You can never tell with our Sterl.'

'I'm going after her,' exclaimed Tamara, suddenly opening the back door and scrambling out of the van.

'Tamara!'

'You can come if you want to, Simon. If not, then shut up!'

'Fuck this,' hissed the detective following the young American out of the van. He'd been given strict instructions by Randolph Sheridan to find his daughter and he wasn't about to let her get killed now. If Sterling wanted to throw away what little remained of her own life then that was her problem. Tamara had to be saved at all costs.

***

'He went that way.'

'Where?' said Simon narrowing his gaze towards where Tamara was pointing.

'Over there between those disused cowsheds — him and

two of his mates; they've followed Sterling into the main part of the farm. Why don't you come over here and see for yourself?'

Simon shifted his position and looked, just in time to see the three men vanish from view as they entered the central group of buildings beyond the cowsheds.

'How did he know where she was?' continued Tamara pondering the situation.

'I haven't got a clue kid, but he's bearing down on Sterling like a hunter-seeker missile and there's nothing we can do to stop him.'

'Maybe there is.'

'How do you mean? He's armed and dangerous and he's got two of his buddies with him. What the hell can *we* do?'

'Follow me, detective,' replied Tamara with a determined gleam in her eye. 'The game's not over yet.'

Sterling moved quickly and silently across the courtyard of the old French farmhouse. She knew Kessler was close. If only she could reach the barn, she stood a good chance of finding some cover and taking him out with a head shot when he passed by. Gripping the handle of her pistol, she edged her way along the wall towards the half-open timber door hoping she hadn't been seen.

Too late—

The unmistakeable figure of David Kessler appeared at the top of the courtyard flanked by two of his goons. She was caught out in the open with nowhere to hide. In vain, she looked around hoping to find a way out of the courtyard. There was a low, brick pig pen at the far end of the yard with an open gateway but it was too far away. At least, too far away for her to make a run for it without coming directly into Kessler's line of fire. What could she do?

In the middle of the courtyard was an abandoned haycart, complete with its cargo of hay bales stacked neatly on top of one another. If she could reach that, she might stand a chance of taking a shot at Kessler, but there was a problem. It was almost the same distance away as the pig pen and not nearly as good cover. She was trapped.

They'd seen it all.

From their vantage point in the upper windows of the farmhouse, Tamara and Simon could see Sterling flatten herself hard against the wall as the bullets came streaming into the courtyard, ricocheting off the flagstones and sides of the farmyard buildings. It was only a matter of time before one of them found its mark.

'I bet he's using silver bullets,' muttered Simon, rubbing his ankle. He'd badly twisted it as they'd crossed a ditch a few minutes before and now it was beginning to hurt like hell.

'I dare say,' replied Tamara pulling her head back in from the open window, 'but Sterling's armed as well. That Glock of hers could pack one heck of a punch if only she could get clear of that wall down there.'

'Yeah — *if only*. If only I had my .38 with me, I could take out those other two guys on either side of Kessler and give Sterling a fighting chance, but I can't. Face it, Tamara, she's finished.'

'Not if I can help it, Simon. I'm going down there.'

'No!'

He was too late. Scarcely had the word left his mouth than he heard Tamara's footsteps thundering down the farmhouse staircase. Then he turned to the window only to witness her running out across the courtyard towards the haycart taking incoming fire from Kessler as she ran.

'Stupid bitch — she'll get herself killed,' Simon heard himself say as he watched the deadly endgame unfold below. He was powerless to do anything about it as the pain in his ankle had increased to such an extent that it rendered any significant movement virtually impossible. All he could do was watch as the bullets from Kessler's machine pistol raked the yard with suppressing fire. Then, just as suddenly as it had started, the firing ceased, leaving everything wrapped in an uneasy silence. Nothing stirred in the courtyard, apart from a few blades of grass caught in the morning breeze which also picked at the remains of the black polythene sheeting still covering some of the hay bales.

'How did you get inside the farmhouse, Tamara?' hissed Sterling across the yard.

'There's a rear entrance through the kitchen at the back. The door wasn't locked so I walked in and Simon followed me.'

'Oh… right.'

'What are we going to do, Sterling?' continued Tamara throwing a stage whisper from the haycart where she'd taken cover.

'You tell me,' answered the vampire, flattening herself closer to the wall. 'That's most likely a MAC-10 Kessler's firing off and I don't know if his mates are packing as well.'

Just then, there came another voice. It was David Kessler. He was standing at the top of the yard levelling the barrel of his machine pistol at them:

'The girl doesn't have to die, Sterling. This is strictly

between you and me.'

'Fuck off, Kessler! Tamara's under my protection.'

'On whose orders?'

'The Vatican's, if you must know.'

'What for?'

'How the fuck should I know? Maybe she's the Second Coming or something. I've learned not to ask too many questions with those bastards.'

'Get your fingers burned, huh?'

'Shut up and back off or I'll put another nail in that left paw of yours.'

'No can do, Sterling,' replied the Dutchman unconsciously stroking the back of his bandaged hand. 'You've challenged my authority in Europe and now I have to demand satisfaction. I have no choice.'

'What's he talking about,' hissed Tamara, still hiding behind the haycart.

'It's a vampire thing,' replied Sterling without taking her eyes off Kessler. 'It appears I've gone and stood on his dick big time and he's pissed off.'

'Oh, I see. Just like real people then?'

'Yeah, just like real people, Tamara. Now shut up and let me concentrate. I think there's going to be a duel.'

'What — you mean like an old Wild West shoot-out? Gunfight at the OK Corral or something?'

'It's not funny, Tamara.'

'I never said it was. Look out, here he comes now—'

Sure enough, David Kessler had detached himself from his two associates and had ordered them to depart. Then he positioned himself within twenty paces of where Sterling was standing by the wall.

'He's calling you out, Sterling. What are you going to do?'

'I've got no choice, kid. I'm going to have to accept the challenge.'

'But he's got a machine gun.'

'Yes, and it's packing silver bullets as well. Don't you think I know that?'

Simon looked on dumbfounded as the deadly gambit unfolded in the courtyard below. There was no way that either of the two women were going to survive the onslaught of a functioning machine pistol like a MAC-10. The only way they stood any chance of getting out alive was if Kessler's gun jammed on him and there was only one chance in a thousand of that ever happening. They were both as good as dead.

Sterling walked slowly into the middle of the courtyard and placed herself in front of the haycart, holding her gun to one side of her at the hip. Then, to his horror, Simon saw Tamara emerge from hiding behind the cart and position herself to the left-hand side of Sterling. 'You'll have to shoot me as well, Kessler,' he heard her say as she took hold of Sterling's free hand and held it in her own.

'Back off,' growled the Dutchman, suspicious of the distraction. 'This is between Sterling and me. It's not for mortals.'

Tamara shook her head and stood her ground, letting go of Sterling's hand and stepping aside to give her friend more freedom to move.

'On a count of three, Kessler!' yelled Sterling checking the safety mechanism of her gun. 'One, two…'

Suddenly, the Dutch vampire thrust out the palm of his hand and cast a surge of energy across the courtyard in Sterling's direction. The shock wave knocked the gun clean out of her hand and sent it spinning across the courtyard close to where Tamara was standing.

She hadn't expected this. Kessler was an alpha vampire like Jimmy Silver, but he was much younger in years. Hardly enough time for him to have evolved the skills necessary to accomplish such a feat, but he had and now her friend was in trouble.

Simon tensed, expecting the worst. Only a miracle could save Sterling now. He was almost on the point of forcing open the window to distract Kessler's attention when he saw something else. It was Ahmed, the young Afghan boy walking into the courtyard from the opposite direction. He must have heard the noise and come over to investigate. In the split second that Kessler took his eyes off Sterling, Tamara picked up the fallen gun and levelled it expertly at the Dutchman, pulling the trigger expertly and without hesitation.

One, two, three, four, five rounds slammed into Kessler's head from close range, completely demolishing his face and causing the back of his skull to explode in a shower of brain and bone fragments. As he fell to the ground, Tamara calmly walked over and put another five rounds into his torso; then, when she was certain he was dead, she handed the gun back to Sterling.

'I think you dropped this,' she said with a smile.

'How did you do that?' exclaimed her companion, open-mouthed with astonishment.

'Because I'm my father's daughter,' replied Tamara, matter-of-factly. Then, glancing up at Simon's face in the window, she continued, '—and because I'm an American.'

No further words were exchanged as the pair stood in the courtyard waiting for Kessler's body to be consumed by the sacred fire. It took longer than they anticipated, but when it came it was quite spectacular, turning his body to ash in less than a minute.

'That'll be me one day,' observed Sterling ruefully.

'Why do you say that?' said the American girl looking down at the rapidly diminishing pile of dust on the courtyard floor.

'Because of the cull, Tamara. The Vatican have ordered a general cull of the Undead in Europe. I thought I'd told you that already.'

'Won't they make an exception in your case?'

'It's unlikely. With Kessler gone, I'm probably number one on their hit list.'

'My father knows people…'

'Yes, but not the right ones. Face it, Tamara, I'm as good as dead already. Come on, let's get back to England and pick up the threads of our lives. There's nothing more we can do here.'

EPILOGUE

'That's an awful lot of aircraft for just one person,' Sterling observed, as the sleek, twelve-seater private executive jet slowly taxied towards them and came to a halt on the tarmac of Heathrow Airport.

'Simon's travelling with me to America,' Tamara replied. 'It's my father's plane. He normally uses it to travel around the States. This is the furthest it's ever been.'

'Oh, right — I see... How's your ankle, Simon?'

'Could have been worse. I think I've just twisted it, that's all. Should be okay in a couple of months or so. How's the boy, by the way?'

'Who — Ahmed?'

'Yes, the young Afghan lad. How is he?'

'Joe took him up to Luton to join his relatives. It was the least we could do for him. After all, he practically saved the day when he blundered into the courtyard like that.'

'What about Spike and Gordon?'

'Gone back to Harlow, I expect. I don't see very much of them these days.'

'And Jerry — how is he?'

'Fine. He's used to these sorts of capers. We go back a long way.'

The side door of the aircraft slowly opened and a short flight of steps descended, gently coming to rest on the tarmac below.

'I think that's our cue,' exclaimed Tamara. 'The pilot wants to be off or he'll lose his place in the line.'

'Yes, Sterling,' echoed Simon. 'We'll have to get a move on. The plane's been cleared for take-off so I guess this is goodbye.'

For a moment, Tamara hesitated, then, plucking up the courage, she kissed Sterling on the cheek trying hard not to wince at the coldness of her flesh.

'Goodbye, Sterling,' she said softly, 'and thanks for everything.'

'Don't mention it, kid. We'll have to do it again sometime, huh?'

The American shook her head with a laugh. 'No, I don't think so. I reckon I've had quite enough of England to last me a lifetime — present company excepted of course.'

Sterling watched as the plane became a distant speck in the sky, carrying Simon and Tamara back to their native land. Turning away, she was about to make for the terminal building when she saw a long, black limousine heading in her direction. As the car drew closer, she turned, expecting the worst, then breathed a sigh of relief when she realised who it was that was sitting in the rear passenger seat.

'Edward!' she exclaimed as the window slowly wound down.

'Who were you expecting?' replied the elderly cleric with a smile, 'an assassination party?'

'Yes, I was rather. The cull is still in force as far as I know.'

'Indeed it is, but not for you.'

'How do you mean?'

The passenger door opened and Cardinal de Valois

stepped out onto the tarmac. He was dressed in his full regalia and looked quite intimidating. As Sterling fell to her knees in respect, the cardinal gestured her to remain standing.

'There is no need for ceremony, my child. You did very well out there in Germany. So much so, that I am pleased to inform you that the Holy Father has granted you a stay of execution — at least for the foreseeable future.'

'How come?'

'As you know, the current pontiff is of a more liberal outlook than his predecessor and is also getting on in years.'

'All popes are getting on in years, Edward. Get to the point.'

'The point is, my dear, that we are in dire need of your services. The increase in the number of vampires in recent years has made it necessary to thin out their ranks a little, and your abilities as an experienced killer has rendered you a person of interest with the Vatican.'

'Are you offering me a job, Edward?'

'Indeed I am, Sterling. My recent appointment to lead the Order of Exorcists has enabled me to put in a good word for you with the powers that be in Rome, and they have agreed to offer you a trial period working for them as their number one vampire hunter. What do you say?'

'Will they give me a free hand to deal with Jimmy Silver?'

'I dare say they will.'

'When can I start?'

'You could start tomorrow, if that's all right with you. There is no salary as such, but I think you will find your claims for expenses more than adequate compensation for your efforts. Your acceptance of the position is entirely at your own risk, of course.'

Sterling considered the cardinal's words carefully then looked him in the eye:

'Very well, Edward; I accept, but only on one condition.'

'And what is that, my child?'

'That you stay off my case for good, is that understood?'

'I will put the matter to the College of Cardinals. I'm sure we can come to some sort of an arrangement.'

'Is it a deal then?'

'It's a deal, Sterling,' replied the cardinal shaking her warmly by the hand. Climbing back into his car, he was about to close the door when he turned to her once again:

'Oh and Sterling; there's just one more thing before I leave…'

'What's that, Edward?'

'Behave yourself. It took an awful lot of influence and persuasion to get you the job.'

'I'll try, Edward,' she answered with a mischievous grin. 'I'll try…'

As the car drove away, Sterling felt a surge of joy and gladness rise up in her heart. For the first time in years, she had a sense of purpose in life and something she could truly call her own. Maybe she did have a future, after all.

About the Author

Ian Robert Bell was born in Newcastle-upon-Tyne, England, in 1955. He studied for an MA degree at York University in 1979 before working as a picture restorer for a number of art galleries and museums in the north of England, including those of the city of Sheffield where he now lives. Though a restorer of paintings by profession, he took up creative writing as his main occupation in 2002 and works primarily in the mystery/thriller end of the literary spectrum. He is also the author of five other books: *Resurrection Blues, London Underground, The Beauty And The Blood, The Black Rose,* and *Black Crows And Cardinals.*

Milton Keynes UK
Ingram Content Group UK Ltd.
UKHW022045101123
432353UK00010B/118